Into the Vortex of Fire

A Story of Honor, Valor, Courage, Sacrifice, and Remembrance

A Novel By James H. Lamason
with Gerard E. Mayers

Foreword by Scott Mingus, Sr.
Maps by Bradley M. Gottfried

DORRANCE
PUBLISHING CO
EST. 1920
PITTSBURGH, PENNSYLVANIA 15238

THE HOURS SAD I LEFT A MAID

A LINGERING FAREWELL TAKING

WHOSE SIGHS AND TEARS MY STEPS DELAYED

I THOUGHT HER HEART WAS BREAKING

IN HURRIED WORDS HER NAME I BLEST

I BREATHED THE VOWS THAT BIND ME

AND TO MY HEART IN ANGUISH PRESSED

THE GIRL I LEFT BEHIND ME ...

– From *The Girl I Left Behind Me,*
a popular Civil War song.

THIS BOOK IS RESPECTFULLY DEDICATED TO
ALL THE GIRLS AND WIVES
LEFT BEHIND BY THE CIVIL WAR.

Some Notable Quotes

Surely my dear, it was a true vortex, of fire and hell
A soldier in a letter home

We have shared the incommunicable experience of war.
We have felt, we still feel the passion of life to its top.
In our youths our hearts were touched with fire!
Oliver Wendell Holmes, Jr.

Men, many a boy here will tell you war is all glory;
boys I tell you, war is all hell!
William T. Sherman

It is good that this (war) is so horrible lest we grow fond of it.
Robert E. Lee, at Fredericksburg, Virginia,
December 13, 1862

Table of Contents

Foreword

Gettysburg

The mere mention of the word conjures up different emotions. For some, it evokes images of the battlefield, adorned for more than 100 years with impressive monuments and markers, making it one of the most impressive collections of outdoor statuary in the world. For others, Gettysburg means a family vacation, filled with battlefield and museum experiences, shopping, dining, and swimming in the hotel's pool. To others, Gettysburg is a place of controversy, with debates lingering over the need for historic preservation versus the desire to add townhouses, retail shopping centers, casinos on occasion, etc.

But to many, the word Gettysburg brings images of something much more personal—the stories of ancestors and kin who fought there, of long-ago warriors from our respective home states, of young men and boys who never came home, many of whom still lie beneath the rich topsoil of Adams County, Pennsylvania. It is the collective stories of thousands of brave (and some not-so-valiant) soldiers, blue and gray, who survived to write their impressions of the three-day battle in their letters home, journals and diaries, newspaper articles, or in memoirs. Several of the soldiers who fought at Gettysburg later were fortunate enough to have the health and means to travel to the former battlefield to attend the dedication ceremonies for their regimental or state monuments, or to visit the graves or the locations where their respective regiments or batteries had once fought.

It is the latter, the stories of the men who were there, those who came back and those who never would, that form the backbone of this work. Author Jim Lamason, long a friend and spiritual brother, and collaborator Gerard Mayers (my co-author of our book of human-interest stories of the Irish in the war) tell the story of one man from New Jersey and his comrades who sweated, toiled, and bled at Gettysburg. This book is a fitting tribute to the sons of New Jersey whose lives were forever changed in the fields that we now know as the Gettysburg National Military Park.

Huzzah.

Scott L. Mingus, Sr.
York, Pennsylvania

Prologue
REMEMBERING

DURING THE EARLY DAYS of June and into the middle of July, of 1863, two great armies (about 170,000 men) marched, covering about a thousand miles in total. They moved from northern Virginia, through or parallel to the Shenandoah Valley, through the heart of Maryland, into south-central Pennsylvania, and then back again.

These two mighty forces left a trail of death and destruction like nothing the people of the United States had ever experienced. It is estimated the armies of the Civil War typically consumed *over 500 tons of food and forage*—for the animals and the men in the ranks—*a day*.

When they finally met at Gettysburg, both the Union Army of the Potomac and the Confederate Army of Northern Virginia consumed so much water that many of the wells within a few miles of the town went dry. It would take a full two months for those wells to completely recover.

Both armies left behind over 7,000 dead animals, which were burned to get rid of them. The stench of that burning lingered in the area for over a month. There are accounts of people in Gettysburg, and in the surrounding areas, who became so seriously ill that many died from the effects.

Then, over 50,000 casualties: 7,000 killed outright; another 35,000 wounded.

The Army of Northern Virginia left the battlefield with its wounded in a wagon train over seventeen miles long. The Confederates and the Army of the Potomac left behind over 27,000 wounded, dying soldiers to be cared for initially by 2,700 people in the town of Gettysburg. That, by the way, is another story in and of itself.

The men of the Eleventh New Jersey Volunteer Infantry regiment were in the middle of all this.

What follows is *their* story. Maybe not so much in their words, but historically backed by many years of research, study, and visits to walk the battlefield.

So, to quote the late 20th-century commentator Paul Harvey, let's tell *the rest of the story*!

Chapter One
AWAKENING THE ECHOES

June, 1888
Somewhere between Trenton, New Jersey,
and Gettysburg, Pennsylvania

"LINES CUT IN imperishable granite, upon the monument which marks this sacred spot, is the record which it submits to posterity, of the part it took to stem the advancing tide of rebellion on the afternoon of July second, 1863."

There! After all this work, the old veteran thought to himself, *there is the centerpiece of this speech.* He'd been working for over an hour in an attempt to convey what he truly wanted to say. He paused for a moment. Colonel John Schoonover looked over at his wife Elizabeth sleeping in the train seat next to him and sighed. As he did so, he realized, with a start, how much time had passed since his last visit to a small college town in south-central Pennsylvania. *Had it really been just over twenty-five years since the battle there at Gettysburg? Had the war to end "the Rebellion" and re-unite the United States truly been over for that long?* He shook his head in astonishment at how swiftly the years flew by. He need only look at his sons and see how fast they had grown. Beholding his reflection in the mirror as he cleaned up at night after work or at the beginning of a new day also spoke volumes.

For Schoonover, this train journey was a culmination and a beginning. It marked the end of a five-year effort to create a fitting monument to his old regiment. Those past five years were busy ones. His personal and professional life had oft intertwined with the plan proposed by the state of New Jersey. In grateful memory to its sons who'd served in the Eleventh New Jersey Volunteer Infantry regiment, the state financed the entire costs associated with the undertaking. His long affiliation with the unit also meant regular communication with the Smith Granite Company, of Westerly, Rhode Island. That was the company selected by the state to fabricate the memorial. Because he'd been the first Adjutant of the regiment, he played not a small part in the monument's ultimate design and its creation. The moment of its dedication was now at hand at last.

The trip was also a beginning. After this journey, no longer would people have to rely solely on the memories of those who'd fought with the regiment and survived the war's black crucible. The dedication of the Eleventh New Jersey's monument at Gettysburg would now, for years to come, enable people to reflect on the courage and sacrifice endured there. Carved in granite in the shape of a large, opened record-book or ledger, the monument also was a memorial for the ages. It was a record for posterity of the part the regiment took on the afternoon of July 2, 1863 to stem the advancing tide of rebellion.

The old veteran's thoughts turned to the recent news about his commanding officer and dear friend, Major General Robert

McAllister. McAllister, once mockingly and then lovingly called *Mother McAllister* by his men, was now on in years. The last report was of the general's ill-health preventing his being present in Gettysburg for the dedication of the regimental monument. Schoonover's mind filled with the memories of all the reunions of the veterans of the war, including the reunions of the old Third Corps, and the other Grand Army of the Republic meetings where McAllister had spoken. He, and McAllister, enjoyed the eternal bond of those who served in the "War of Rebellion," as the general referred to it. They truly had been, and to some extent still were, comrades in arms.

A sly smile creased John's face as he recalled the general's subsequent treatment at Gettysburg after being severely wounded. The loud chuckle it drew from him roused his wife from sleep. It caused her to stir in the seat beside him.

Sitting up and brushing the sleep from her eyes, Elizabeth said, "My dear John, what *are* you laughing at?" Remembering John's telling her of the episode, she said, "Oh, that story *again!!*" Hooking her hand around his arm, she chuckled also. "He is such a dear man, isn't he?"

"Yes, my dear," Schoonover answered, "and that story just speaks of the man. And it shows he was well, human, too!"

Another chortle came from the back of his throat. Elizabeth said, "Okay, *out with it!* What struck you so funny now? Not the same story, is it?"

"No," Schoonover replied to his wife. "I was thinking of the first time the regiment was being drilled. And how the general would be watching us, cajoling the men, *prodding* them to get the drill right. How soon after, the men called him *Mother McAllister*, because he looked to every detail, was at every drill time, even led a number of them. How he would sometimes gently, or sometimes with that baritone voice of his—which all of us later on learned could be heard above the roar of battle—admonish us! But there was never a curse word, never a word said in unkindness. Yes, he could be... well, a martinet, but it was for their good, for our good. Even the officers."

Even the officers...including me, he thought to himself. *Even me.* In response, a tear slowly ran down his cheek.

"You know, my dear," he said, sniffling back that tear and clearing his throat, "that nickname went from being a name said under men's breath, almost derisive, to a term of endearment. Almost to the point of, well, deep affection toward him. For they realized, *we all realized* he did it so we would have a better chance to survive. And we all owe him a debt of thanks. All of us..."

He fell silent, thinking to himself as he watched the fields and trees roll on by. *Even me,* again he thought. *Even for me.* He burst into sobs.

Elizabeth was startled by this. She had never seen him cry like this before. "John, John, *John!*" He collapsed onto her shoulder, burying his face in it. She held him close; he slowly but surely regained control.

"Sorry my dear, those memories of him, and especially Gettysburg, just over-whelmed me." Schoonover blew his nose and regained his composure.

"John," Elizabeth said, "you told me you must finish your speech."

He shifted uneasily in his seat. Ever since those long-ago days during the Battle of the Wilderness in early May of 1864, his health had not been robust. In fact, one of his illnesses caused him great discomfort whenever he sat anywhere for long. His ill-health often left him feeling frail, and at times, exhausted. Schoonover nodded his head at his wife's admonition. In doing so, those faces, the faces of McAllister, Martin, Lloyd, Ackerman, Faussett, Kearny, and finally one more…a young private, all flashed through his mind. *What was that young man's name? Mountain? Mount? Ah yes, Jake Mount! I will get back to the speech, but I must rest first. Yes, sleep will help me focus.* With the faces of his comrades still spinning in his mind and memory, and the words "Lines cut in imperishable granite" echoing in his brain, he drifted off to sleep….

August 25, 1862
Camp Perrine
The Eleventh Regiment, New Jersey Volunteer Infantry
Near Trenton, New Jersey

A blaring horn's harsh sound rocked John Schoonover out of the soundest night's sleep he'd had in weeks. Wiping the sleep from his eyes, he slowly sat up on his cot. As he sat there, moving his head from side to side, and stretching the last vestiges of sleep away, the smell of coffee met his nostrils. That, and the wonderful smell of breakfast being cooked, made his stomach rumble.

Hmmm, he thought to himself. *This is going to be a wonderful morning of breakfast!* With a shock, he realized, *Oh no! This is the final day of camp! I am not at home; I am the Adjutant for the regiment! I should be up already! What is the Colonel to say?!?*

Schoonover bedded down the night before in his white muslin three-button placket long-sleeved shirt, his sky-blue kersey woolen trousers, and his cotton stockings. Slipping on his boots and quickly grabbing his red infantry officer's sash, he shrugged into his single-breasted dark blue officer's frock coat with shoulder boards denoting his rank as a First Lieutenant and buttoned it up. Wrapping the sash about his waist in the prescribed fashion, he then checked to make sure it was properly placed. The young officer next reached for his belt and sword, buckling them on. A quick glance in the small mirror hanging on his tent pole showed him to be presentable. *Damn it man, you should have taken more time!* One more quick splash of water on his face and he carefully opened the tent flap to peer out at the scene before him.

Standing *right there* with coffee in his hand was the colonel, Robert McAllister. The lieutenant colonel, Stephen Moore, stood beside him. Their backs were to Schoonover, with McAllister being a slight bit taller than Moore. Schoonover found himself hoping and praying that neither of his senior officers saw him.

The first words from McAllister were said almost in a growl. "You are *late*, Mister Schoonover!" Schoonover thought to himself, *How in the world did he??*

"Begging the Colonel's pardon, but I was seeing to some of my duties…and…and…" Schoonover's voice trailed off, totally flustered. McAllister spun on his heels; Moore right behind him.

"Sir, I hope the duties of reading the inside of your eyelids were beneficial and the task accomplished!" To the young adjutant, it seemed as if McAllister's eyes bore right through him. Then a slight smile creased the side of the colonel's mouth.

Schoonover was confused. When he first stepped out, he thought he was going to get a dressing down. Now, that slight smile. *What's going on here?*

Of the three, two of them had served together since the First New Jersey Regiment of Volunteer Infantry days. Lt. Colonel Moore had been with the Third New Jersey Regiment of Militia. He had come over to the Eleventh and mustered in on August 14, 1862. McAllister and Schoonover were veterans of McClellan's Peninsula Campaign in the spring of that year; Moore was a veteran of the first real campaign of the war, culminating with the first Battle of Bull Run. During the Peninsula Campaign, Schoonover had been a private in the First New Jersey, rising to the rank of commissary sergeant. When the Eleventh New Jersey was formed, McAllister asked for him *by name*. The leadership of the Eleventh were all experienced in the art of war. In addition to Schoonover, the roster of those from the old First New Jersey included some of the junior officers and sergeants from that regiment. William J. Mount, the acting regimental sergeant major, had served as a sergeant with Lt. Colonel Moore in the old Third New Jersey Militia.

Schoonover snapped to attention and saluted. *How do I recover from this one,* he thought. *Oh man, am I in for it!*

"Begging the Colonel's pardon, sir, but…yes, sir, I was doing just that sir, finest night's sleep I had in a long while, sir! Um, sir…I hope you slept well, too!" He stood there, holding the salute, waiting for it to be returned.

McAllister also came to attention, snapped off a return salute, and then came face to face with Schoonover. Their faces almost touching, Schoonover smelled the coffee breath of his superior officer. Noticing that the colonel's eyes had narrowed to slits like piercing arrows, the young officer waited for his commander to speak.

"I had a fine night's sleep," McAllister replied, "thank you for asking." A slight growling expression crunched his face, with his eyes dancing. "But understand this, mister! From now on, you *will* be up *with me*, and will join me before the regiment is up! Do you understand me?"

Schoonover gulped, almost shaking in his boots.

"Sir! Begging the colonel's pardon, sir; it will never happen again! Sir!" The words rolled off his tongue almost automatically. "My profoundest apologies, sir!"

Almost spitting out his next words, McAllister replied: "Don't *ever* apologize to me again, mister! It's a sign of weakness! Understood?!?"

Schoonover blinked; once, twice, three times. "Yes, sir; never apologize."

McAllister went on. "Lieutenant, you are part of this regiment's leadership. You have earned your rank by service to the First New Jersey, to the State of New Jersey, *and* to the cause of preserving the Union! You will conduct yourself accordingly! Understood?"

His voice almost quivering, Schoonover responded, "Yes, sir; thank you, sir. Never apologize again, sir; so, noted…"

McAllister smiled, and then continued: "Now that we understand each other, Mr. Schoonover, you will have the *Officers' Call* sounded. Once all the officers are gathered here, and all present, you will cause the Long Roll for Assembly beat by the drummers, and buglers to sound *Reveille*, and the regiment to fall in for Inspection."

Schoonover nodded as he heard this. Satisfied the young adjutant understood, McAllister went on, softening his tone slightly. "After all, this is our official muster-in day. We are to receive our colors from Governor Olden, and then break camp. By the end of today we are headed to Washington City to join the Army of the Potomac. See to it, Mister!"

Thoroughly confused now, Schoonover did nothing but stammer out, "Yes sir, *Officers' Call*, Long Roll, buglers to sound *Reveille*, officers to get their companies moving! Will do, sir!" He came to attention and snapped off a solid salute to his commanding officer; to which McAllister replied. With a hasty "With your permission, Colonel," off he went.

McAllister said to Moore, "Hmm, I do think there is hope for that young man! He could be a fine leader of men someday, don't you think, Moore?"

Moore smiled, took a long pull on his pipe, nodded with a smirk, said, "Yes, there is hope for him, yet!" They both chuckled.

Schoonover ran what just happened to him through his mind. He thought to himself, *why didn't I choose my words more carefully? After all, the colonel* did *ask for me by name…*Continuing, he thought, *Yes, I am in a different position now. If the regiment ever got in a tight spot, I could be in command.* That very thought sent a chill down his spine. *No! No! Never happen! The colonel will* never *let it happen! All will be well, and I* must *learn to do my job!*

As he finished the thought, he literally ran right into Captain Philip Kearny, commanding Company A of the regiment.

"Hey, Schoonover! Watch where you are going! Why such a hurry?"

"Sorry, Captain," Schoonover replied, as he picked himself up and dusted off his uniform and sash. "I was thinking about what I have to do right now."

As if a smirk was forming, one side of Kearny's face upturned slightly. "I could not help overhearing what happened with you and the Colonel. Rattled you a good bit, if I heard rightly."

"With all due respects, Captain," Schoonover responded, "yes, it was hard, but it was well deserved. He was right; I was wrong. It is over. And…and I have learned from it!"

"Yes, you did," Kearny said, "but I would have handled it a bit differently. But, as you say, it's over now. You have a message for me?"

Coming to attention, Schoonover gave Kearny the message of *Officers' Call.* Continuing, he said, "After *Officers' Call* is sounded, the First Sergeants are to bring their companies on line. The front of their company tent line is where they are to fall in, with all their equipment, sir!" The young adjutant saluted the other officer after delivering the message.

Kearny returned the salute. "Thank you, Lieutenant; I will see to my company." Thinking to himself, Kearny noted, *Yes, I would have handled it better. Well, off to it.* He moved away to inform his first sergeant the men needed to be up and moving. After that, he turned toward where McAllister and Moore took position.

Within moments, a bugle sounded the *Officers' Call* and then *First Call,* echoed by the regimental drummers. The training camp of the Eleventh came fully to life. Each soldier made sure he had proper placement of all his accoutrements — cap box in proper place on the waist belt, bayonet scabbard near the left hip, cartridge box on its sling properly placed on the right hip under the waist belt, every button properly buttoned, and the kepi in proper position. Important also was the correct position of the soldier's haversack on the left hip under the waist belt, and the essential canteen above it. No packs yet, that would come; they all knew the Colonel was going to inspect them this morning. All the training was over. These young men, the majority of them with an average age of twenty (with a good number still just barely seventeen), knew today was a *very* special one indeed.

Privates Joseph Cheston, Jacob Mount, and William Fraley of Co. C helped each other with making sure their equipment was properly set. All of them were about the same age — just over seventeen. Their teenage boyhood and sense of adventure was written all over their faces. The exuberance of youth being away from home for the first time and of being part of something bigger, and much larger than themselves was plainly evident. Both Joey and Jake had girls back home; and yes, this was a way to impress their sweethearts.

The enlisted men in the regiment came from all walks of life. Some had been shop-keepers, bookkeepers, farm hands, laborers and even just boys. Looking for adventure. They had answered Lincoln's call for 300,000 more troops to put down "the rebellion" — as McAllister and the officers of the regiment referred to it. But, under the ever-watchful eye of their colonel, they quickly learned every button better be properly in place, every piece of equipment clean and ready for action, and every part of the drill better be *exactly* the way the colonel wanted it. Now, on this day of days, they felt they were ready. As the men and officers of the Eleventh fell in, they felt no small measure of pride and confidence.

Eight-hundred-and-seventy-six officers and men would leave Camp Perrine, their Camp of Instruction, this day. The deserters, the shirkers, the medically unfit, were gone — weeded out by McAllister's unflinching exactness and discipline.

One by one, each company fell into line in front of its company street. As each company formed up, it held itself in readiness for the next commands. Once each company was aligned into two ranks and properly counted off, it came to attention. The roll call was then taken by each company's first sergeant. Before each company were the arms they'd stacked the night before. After taking their places, the men waited behind their stacked arms. At the command to *"Take Arms,"* the men took their weapons and came to the position of arms at the shoulder, and at attention.

The next order was the one they all waited for. The senior lieutenant of each company bellowed out, *"Attention, Com-*

pany! Right Face!" At this order, each company automatically turned from a double line into a marching column of four men abreast. At the command of *"Right Shoulder Shift, Arms! By the left flank, Forward, March!"*, each company moved off by the left flank to the parade ground. There, each company was met by its commanding officer, a captain. Under his guidance, each company then prepared for the next part of the inspection ceremony.

Schoonover watched this all with almost rapt awe. He remembered how badly they looked when they started their training. *Hell, most of them did not know their right from their left.* Collisions on the field during drill at times had been almost chaotic! If not downright hilarious. But over time they got it. As each company marched up to the parade ground and took its proper placement in the regimental line, it was amazing how smooth and with careful precision all of this was executed. Schoonover noticed how each company carefully dressed itself on its right flank guidon marker. They were dressed, left to right, Company A, B, D, E, C, F, G, H, I, and K. The color company this day was C. That meant its position was at the center of the regimental line. The nine men from the company who would be the color guard stepped to the front of the regiment, halted, and waited.

"They are a regiment now, ready to fight — or at least they think so," Schoonover thought to himself as he stood there at his proper post.

Once each company was properly placed, the first sergeant then reported to the captain of the company being present and accounted for. As the designation for each company was called, that company's first sergeant stepped forward, saluted, and reported to the Adjutant, "All present and accounted for, sir!" No one was going to miss today, not even those who'd been sick or in the infirmary. It was just *too* special a day indeed.

When all the companies reported in, McAllister stepped forward after drawing his sword and placing it against his right shoulder. Rapping out a series of commands, he bellowed, *"Attention, Battalion! Fix, Bayonets! Shoulder, Arms! Right Shoulder Shift, Arms! Order, Arms! Parade, Rest!"* At each command, there came the sound of bayonets hissing from their scabbards, being placed with a clink and clatter on the muskets, weapons to the right shoulder, then down to the side, and placed in the position of parade rest. All were in readiness to hear what the colonel would say next. All this done smoothly, in unison, as if the entire regiment was a single, living creature.

"Good morning, men and officers of the Eleventh Regiment!" McAllister then said. "As you all know, today is a most important one for all of us! All of your training, all of your preparation, has led us, each of us, to this day! I am proud of all of you!"

At a nod from McAllister, Schoonover then took over. *"Attention, Battalion! Prepare for Inspection!"* Looking up and down the regimental line, he then commanded, *"To the Rear, in Open Order, March!"* At that the sergeants of the companies marched a prescribed number of paces to the rear, with the rear ranks of the companies then following. When all the rear ranks were ready, the sergeants then resumed their own proper placement in line.

That finished, McAllister with Moore, Major Valentine Mutchler, and Schoonover (plus each company's commander) began the review of each company by rank. Front row first. With pencil and paper in hand, Schoonover took notes as to each soldier's name and then beside it any remarks. A button missing, to be replaced. Or maybe the cartridge box did not look clean. Or maybe there was a problem with the percussion cap lock or trigger of the musket. The interesting thing in all this there was no screaming or the colonel getting in their faces that this or that needed correction. It was all as if he was their father or big brother or just that older person who gently but with strong voice let them know what should be.

Finally, Inspection Arms was done. The rear ranks of all the companies received the command to rejoin the front ranks. Then, when the regiment was again run through the Manual of Arms, it was dismissed by company. Now it was time for breakfast.

McAllister retired to his tent and removed his hat plus his sword and sash.

Commissary Sergeant Philip Crisp approached the colonels with a cup of hot coffee with a plate full of bacon, eggs, and a biscuit for each. As he handed the plates over, he smiled.

"Colonel, sir, with the compliments of all of us, here is some breakfast to help you on a busy day! And, for you too, Colonel Moore, as well! Enjoy, gentlemen!"

"And a heartfelt thank you to you, sergeant, as well," McAllister said. "See to yourself, sir!"

As the commissary sergeant turned to leave, McAllister called after him. "Oh, and please be sure to let Mr. Schoonover know he is requested to join us for break-fast! And, sir, see to it that he receives the same as us!"

"Yes, Colonel; right away, Colonel!"

Looking at his second in command, McAllister asked, "Well, what do you think of today thus far? Splendid, I say; *splendid!*"

Moore took a pull on his pipe and let out a long, slow puff of smoke. Smiling broadly, he replied, "Yes, Colonel, a feast that is sure to get us through this day, indeed!"

Both men dug in. As they ate, they noticed the rest of camp lined up at the commissary wagons. McAllister noted, "They should eat as much as they all can get. It is going to be a long time before they eat like this again. Right, Stephen?"

"Yes," Moore said, in between bites of his food. "Remember, sir, when we mustered in the other regiments before? Some of the men would refuse to eat or were too sick to do so! At least *this* unit seems a bit fitter, a bit hungrier…But the last time we went through this, some of the men didn't eat for days."

"Unfortunately, yes," McAllister replied. "I don't know…" He fell silent for a moment.

Moore put his fork down and asked, "What's wrong, sir? What are your thoughts?"

"I was just thinking of the men of the First New Jersey," McAllister continued after a short pause. "How they served so valiantly, with purpose and courage, especially during the battles back down the Peninsula with McClellan. Surely you remember, Stephen, the battle of First Bull Run. Oh, what sacrifice, and bloodletting! Just an incredible time. *Incredible.* Those dear men, oh, such courage…." His voice trailed off.

Moore put down his fork. "Colonel, sir, that was a courageous time and an incredible time, indeed! But, sir, we cannot dwell on that; we must look forward, sir, to do as you always tell us, to…to press on!"

Before McAllister could reply, Acting Sgt. Major William J. Mount appeared and saluted. "Begging the Colonel's pardon! Sir, our guests have arrived. They are here! Governor Olden has also come with them!"

McAllister stood up and returned the salute. "Thank you, Sergeant Major, please tend to their needs. Water, perhaps?"

"Yes, sir," Mount replied.

"We shall all be on the parade ground shortly, Mr. Mount." Dismissing the Sergeant Major, McAllister called out, "Schoonover!"

Schoonover seemed to appear out of nowhere, vainly trying to swallow a big mouthful of his breakfast. "Colonel, sir; what is your pleasure, sir?"

"Mr. Schoonover," McAllister said after looking at his pocket watch, "please have the company commanders order their men to fall in, in about…oh, fifteen minutes." McAllister thought to himself, I *must let the men finish eating at least! And remind them to do right on the parade ground; we must not keep our guests waiting too long.* To Schoonover again, he said: "Hold on a moment. After about fifteen minutes, so the men can finish their breakfasts, have the Long Roll beaten and *Officers' Call* sounded. The men should fall in on the parade ground. Colonel Moore and I will be there forthwith. "

"Sir!" With a "By your leave," the young adjutant turned on his heels and headed toward the company commanders, and then to the musicians to carry out his orders.

Both the colonel and Moore finished their meal, put their coats and sashes back on, checked to see if their swords were on correctly, checked each other to make sure their hats were on *just so.* They saluted each other and then stepped out onto the parade ground together.

By now, the entire regiment had assembled on the parade ground. The first sergeants of each company checked to make sure all were present, and reported to their senior lieutenants all present and accounted for; the senior lieutenant then reported to his captain.

At a cue from McAllister, Moore called them to attention. *"Attention, Battalion! Shoulder, Arms! Order, Arms! Parrrade, Rest!"*

Out of the background stepped Governor Charles Smith Olden. A short man with bristly mutton chop whiskers which were gray in color, speckled with black mixed in, Olden made his way up to where McAllister and Moore stood, waiting. A stovepipe type hat sat rather jauntily on his head, almost to say he was the most important person of the day.

Moore called out, *"Prrresent, Arms!"* With precision and a rattle of equipment, the entire regiment came to the proper position to render honors to a visiting dignitary or to a superior commanding officer, such as the general of their brigade.

With the Governor was his wife Phoebe, an aide, and a couple of other state officials looking like they, too, had the air of self-importance that on this day really didn't matter. Only what was *about* to happen was the true purpose of it all.

Olden stepped over to McAllister, who turned and rendered a salute. "Colonel McAllister, I present to you on behalf of the good citizens of the United States and the people of New Jersey, your State Colors!" The military aide with Olden stepped forward to give the colors to Olden, who then presented them to McAllister. Again, the Colonel snapped a salute, and received the colors.

McAllister turned briskly and handed the colors to Mount, who in turn gave a quick salute, about faced, and in turn handed them to Captain John Willis of Company C. With another return of a crisp salute, Willis then handed the state color to the lead sergeant of the color guard, who stepped backward, clutching the flag in his hands.

Turning toward his military aide again, Olden continued, "Colonel McAllister, it is my honor now to present to you, again on behalf of the people of New Jersey and of these

United States, your National Colors. I am sure your regiment will not only do the Nation proud, but also the people of New Jersey whom you serve! Carry them with the blessing and best wishes of your countrymen!"

With that, with a crisp salute McAllister received the national colors. As before, the national colors were handed to Sergeant Major Mount, who in turned gave them to Willis, who passed the colors to the sergeant of the color guard. A proper salute followed each handover. Finally, the regiment now had all its colors in its possession.

Pulling his sword from the scabbard, and placing it on his right shoulder, McAllister about faced. Facing the assembled men of the regiment, and in the loudest and sternest voice he could muster, he said, "Captain Willis! You will have the men of the color guard uncover the colors!!!"

Willis raised his sword from his right shoulder. With the flat of the blade, he slowly raised it to his nose in the position of "Present, Arms." And then slowly returned it. He spun on his heels with a distinct about face. The moment the regiment had been working toward for over a month was now here. "Sergeant," Willis ordered, "you will uncover the colors!" The order no sooner left his lips that the cover on the colors was pulled and the flags unfurled. A breeze picked up at that very moment, causing the flags to unfold as a new bed sheet would do on a warm summer's day. Revealed were the star field on the National flag, and the eagles of the United States Army on the State flag. The blue in the State flag never seemed bluer than at that moment, matching the deep blue sky that hovered over them. The National flag, whose red and white stripes would never again seem to be as deep a red and the white never whiter, caught the breeze. Suddenly, clouds appeared overhead. For a slight moment a ray of sun light bathed the whole scene in a white light, focusing on the color guard. Framing it even the more so in the bright sun of the day.

At that moment, the band struck up "Hail to the Chief," and marched in front of the regiment and the assembled dignitaries. The order to *"Right shoulder shift, Arms!"* rang out. The regiment as one shifted the weapons up to the right shoulders from the previous position of arms at the shoulder.

As the band passed the color guard, the order came for the guard to do a left wheel; they, too, fell in behind the band. With Company C in the van, one by one, the other companies followed suit to pass in review before the regimental field staff and the assembled dignitaries. Each captain had already ordered his company to form a column of fours and prepare to pass in review. As each company passed the assembled dignitaries, the order *"Eyes, right!"* rang out. Each company commander presented his sword in the prescribed manner of the flat blade of his sword to his nose as he passed by, and then back to the shoulder. Each company also moved from the position of right shoulder shift arms to the position of *"Present, Arms"* and then back to the shoulder as it passed. As each company cleared the reviewing area, it was ordered back to eyes front. Eventually, the entire regiment marched by. Company K being the last, the band (which had returned to the middle of the field in front of the officers) finished up its playing.

Once returned to proper positions on the parade ground, the entire regiment, now with its set of colors, received the order for dismissal from Lt. Colonel Moore. Each company then returned to its company street, stacked arms, was dismissed, and began the process of breaking camp.

It was time. The time for training was over; no more exercises of this sort were needed. The pageantry, the glorious part, was done. Honors had been rendered. They had their colors. It was time to get down to the real reason for all of this. It was time for the dirty, unrelenting, vicious duty of war. It was time to test all their training. Only time would tell if they were truly ready. Next stop…Washington City. And then? Onward to the Army of the Potomac, the army the regiment would fight in, would bleed in, and die in…for three long years.

They were on their way.

Chapter Two
R & R

Aboard the train...

S C R E E E E E E C H H H H ... Schoonover jolted awake. Had he dreamed all of that, again? Relived it all again?

He sat up, rubbing his eyes to clear the sleep from them. Though she had moved to the seat across from him, his wife Elizabeth was still dozing. Their two sons Frank and John Depue were also sleeping, leaning on their mother.

Where were they? he thought to himself. The conductor (who'd just come aboard at that stop) made his way down the aisle, announcing the station. "Allentown this stop, Allentown..."

Schoonover was still waking up when the conductor asked him for his tickets. "Ahhh, headed to Gettysburg I see.... Big goings on there I hear."

Schoonover smiled. "Yes, we are unveiling and dedicating the monuments to the memories of the men from New Jersey who gave their all in the service of the United States and their home state."

The conductor nodded his head, punched all their tickets, and then moved on. John sighed. It was a sigh of a combination of things. Of the weariness that lingered over him; of a sense that even now, just twenty-five years after the conclusion of the battle, the Civil War was very quickly getting shoved into the back reaches of the overall conscientiousness of the people of the United States. As if the nation collectively wanted to forget those four horrible, bloody years, and move on. Though the generation that served during it — or lived during it — still remembered it, to the new generation it was now becoming…well, a bit blasé.

Schoonover thought of the parades he went to on Memorial Day, or even the Grand Army of the Republic meetings. And how even now, the numbers of those who survived diminished on an ever-quickening pace. So, it was very important that they get these monuments dedicated *now,* while there was still a sizable number of veterans still alive.

Schoonover took a deep breath and let it out slowly. *"It's time to get back to the speech."* He again pulled out the paper and re-read what he'd written so far. Writing this speech was turning into a chore. Weighted down once again with heaviness because McAllister would not be there for the dedication. That made what he had to do that much more difficult. *How do I work his valiant service into this without sounding well, sad?*

In addition, there were the thoughts once again of those who had died in the battle or even the whole war. Their faces just danced before him. Even Kearny, whose letters home to his mother about how he thought he could have done a better job commanding the regiment were posthumously published. Then McAllister's gracious reply. All of this ran through his head.

The conductor's shout of *All aboooaarrddd!!* and the two whistles brought him out of his musings; in fact, it made him jump. *Well, back to it. I must get back to it….*

June 19, 1863

Gum Springs, Va.

180 miles from Gettysburg, Pennsylvania.

He was tired; so very tired. The rain that had been off and on most of the march calmed the dust down and made it easier to push on. Colonel Robert McAllister pulled a handkerchief from the inside of his coat pocket and wiped the perspiration from his face. Now just over fifty years old, his young-looking face hid his age well. The only telltale signs were the streaks of gray in his full head of hair and the crow's feet around his eyes that come with age. Physically well-built and in great shape, he carried himself well. Though now as he walked with his men, his back was aching along with his sore feet.

Regimental adjutant John Schoonover was by his side. Schoonover handed him the orders just received from their brigade commander Brigadier General Joseph B. Carr. They were to stop ahead in the fields to the right of the road. McAllister nodded at Schoonover. "Pass the word to the company commanders that we will be taking a break and to keep the men together. No camp-fires yet; it's expected this break would only be a short one."

How many miles had they come in the last few days? Had it been days? Right now it seemed like months *that they had been on the road since they left the Rappahannock River.* McAllister snapped out of his reverie; it was time to get off the road. The sun's rays were fading away. He instructed the color sergeant to have the color guard follow him into the pasture.

Leading his horse Old Charlie by its reins, he pushed open the gate into the field. He slowly headed for the grouping of pine trees on the other side. As he wanted to set the standard for his proud regiment, McAllister straightened his coat and assumed an erect bearing. Since the regiment marched in the van of the rest of the brigade, he wanted to set the example. Despite their weariness, the men behind him caught the action of their colonel. They fell into step, under a good strong cadence.

McAllister found the spot he desired. Halting the column, he saw the company commanders already preparing to transition the entire regiment from marching column of fours to company line. The regiment finally stopped. Under his watchful eye, the transition went smoothly. Despite the miles they had covered, these veterans did it automatically! Little fanfare, little confusion. Moving from the position of right shoulder shift arms for the march to shouldered arms, the company commanders gave the order to go from this position to ordered arms and finally parade rest. And it was done quickly and efficiently. The colonel smiled to himself and made note of this to share his satisfaction with the officers in the meeting shortly to follow.

As McAllister looked at the entire regiment assembled before him, he cleared his voice, and said, "Men, we have come a long way; however it is most likely we shall continue this march together shortly. So, get off your feet, no fires yet, and get some water in you. Major Kearny! You will dismiss the regiment with my compliments and have the officers meet with me over by that tree," he pointed at the chosen object, "in five minutes."

He handed his reins to Sergeant Major Henry C. Tilton and then headed to the tree. Slowly he sank to the ground and removed his boots. As he did so, the officers began to gather around him.

First to approach was Captain Andrew Ackerman. A quiet man who knew his job. In battle courageous to a fault, but his men would follow him anywhere. He shared McAllister's love of the Bible and deeply appreciated the colonel's quiet encouragement.

Next to approach was Major Philip Kearny. Second in command with the illness of Lt. Colonel Stephen Moore, his uncle was the late Major General Philip Kearny who was killed the fall before at Ox Hill. Kearny was young, just recently promoted to major at McAllister's urgent request. Being so young, he was given to being a bit of a braggart. To some of his brother officers, he seemed — at times — to try to live up to his uncle's reputation. He had, however, shown at Chancellorsville to be a steady, fierce, and courageous leader of men.

Next were Captains Dorastus Logan and Luther Martin, and First Lt. John Schoonover. All were chatting and going back and forth over something deep. Logan loved to talk with his hands. When it came to politics and the whole reasons for the "Rebellion," his eyes flashed. Schoonover was the unruffled one; he'd been exposed for the first time at Chancellorsville to serious combat as the regimental adjutant. He'd acquitted himself well. The rest of the officers drifted in, including Edward Welling, the regimental surgeon.

"Be seated, gentlemen, and make yourselves as comfortable as possible," was McAllister's comment. "Let us give thanks to our God for a safe journey thus far and pray for safekeeping in the coming battle." Everyone then present bowed their heads as the colonel fervently gave thanks.

The short prayer over, the meeting commenced. "Gentlemen, this will most likely be another short rest. I know we are all tired, but as we all know the enemy is somewhere to our north. And we are pursuing him with all possible speed.

Also, I want to compliment you all on how well we transition from column of fours to company line, and from shoulder shift arms, to shoulder arms, to ordered arms, and then to parade rest. Well done!" In different ways the officers either muttered their "thank you, sir" or stirred somewhat uncomfortably.

"Well, gentlemen, we know from the activities of our cavalry of the last few days, our enemy is being located. Where the Rebs are right now, is open to conjecture. But I do suspect we will be fighting a major battle shortly. Enough of that. Doctor, do you have a medical report for us?"

Surgeon Welling stepped forward, clad in a dirty white flowing coat, his glasses lower down on the bridge of his nose, his hair matted by sweat. Clearing his throat, he said, "We have a few men who are sick with the usual cases of not *enough* water and *too much* fresh fruit. Other than that, and we *all* are foot sore (there were various mumbles and chuckles in agreement) — coupled with a blistered foot here and there, we are in good shape."

Captain Ackerman cleared his throat as a means of shifting the conversation in his direction. "Our straggling has been not as bad as in the past, even as the rest of the brigade." The officers all knew the reason for that; the Eleventh New Jersey was by now a veteran regiment of volunteers. Three hundred-plus souls strong. They had seen it all since they mustered in not quite a year ago.

McAllister nodded. At that moment, the sergeant major stepped into the group. "With the colonel's pardon, I have updated orders." He handed the paper with the orders to McAllister, who'd risen to his feet. A crisp salute followed.

"Thank you, Sergeant Major."

"Well, gentlemen," McAllister said, after a quick perusal, "it seems we are to remain here for the rest of the day. So, with that, please return to your companies and see to it that the men are able to eat something and go ahead and light the camp-fires." To Kearny, McAllister noted, "Major, would you please see to it that the companies are laid out in our usual custom."

With that, the short meeting was over. "See to your men, gentlemen; and I will be around shortly. Mr. Schoonover, would you please stay here for a moment?"

Schoonover sat down next to the colonel. Over the now almost eighteen months they had been together, he had grown to admire McAllister. He chuckled to himself at a memory of how the men called him *Mother McAllister* due to his refusal to drink the hard stuff, and they used to grumble at his strict disciplinary ways, insisting on drill and *more* drill. Also, that they took good care of their muskets, their clothes, especially their shoes, and finally their feet. This perception was beginning to soften though. *Interesting,* he thought to himself.

"John, we must get started."

At McAllister's reminder, Schoonover snapped out of his moment of daydreaming. The colonel then asked for a review of the current state of supplies, including ammunition and foodstuffs. The regiment was in good shape overall, Schoonover reported.

"So, how are you?" McAllister asked.

Via the flickering light from the nearby bright camp-fire, Schoonover looked into the face of his commander and noticed how tired even *he* looked. The weariness they all felt was obvious even now on McAllister's own face. It had aged the colonel.

"A bit foot sore," Schoonover replied, "but I am all right. I am more worried about *you,* sir!"

McAllister sighed. A heavy, bone-weary sigh. "Yes, it's been hard on me, and well, I don't want to complain, but the miles we have added in the last few days have taken a toll on this old man." A weary smile crossed his face. "Well, Lieutenant, we must see to the men. And you need to get some food as well."

With that Schoonover got up and saluted his commander. Saying "with your permission, sir," he walked away to see to his duties.

As McAllister watched the younger man leave, he recalled the day when the regiment was mustered into service. He smiled at the memory. *"He has come a long way since that day. And yes, he has become a fine officer."* He found himself reflecting on the battle of Chancellorsville where Schoonover had more than shown he was there. *If we get in a tight spot my only concern will be, can he lead all of them?* For this battle-hardened veteran, *that* thought sent a chill up his back. *Yes, that would mean I have lost my fight…But that is all in God's hands.* And he sighed. *I cannot worry about that.*

"Sergeant," he called out to his commissary sergeant. "How are we doing with something to eat? How is the coffee coming?"

"In a moment, sir!" was the reply.

Good, McAllister thought to himself, *I have time for a letter.* He reached over and pulled his saddlebag to him, retrieved a couple of sheets of paper, and a pencil. Shrugging his shoulders and working the kinks out of his neck and back, he began to write. Licking the tip of his pencil, he paused. Trying to find the words to begin. Like the many others he had written the months before, it began with its standard opening of *My dear Ellen, and family.* He proceeded to go on about the march, and how they were now in pursuit of the Army of Northern Virginia. The many miles they had come, particularly the hard march on the fifteenth. The command began its movement that day at one in the afternoon, in intense heat, and not halting until almost midnight.

The fits and stops of the last few days, affording some opportunities for rest, made for easier marching. Nevertheless, the men seemed to be in good spirits. As he worked on the letter, Sgt. Crisp stepped forward.

"Colonel, me darling, here is your coffee, sir. And some corn bread."

"Thank you, Sergeant; please see to yourself."

"Certainly, sir. And you are welcome." With a nod of acknowledgment, the sergeant returned to his fire and further cooking.

Back to his writing. In between sips of the hot, welcome liquid and munch of the cornbread, he told his family he is well. And that he would write again soon. Suddenly he noticed it was getting quite dark. *Hmm, time to close this.* With that thought, he finished the letter, sealed it in an envelope, and addressed it to his wife.

Time to get his bedroll, blanket, and pillow out. He thought for a moment. *I should really visit the men. Really should. But I am so tired. So tired. Ah, yes, let me lie here for a moment or two.*

Commissary Sergeant Crisp was cleaning up when he heard it. The sound of a very tired person. He walked over to the colonel. He was sound asleep. And with that, Crisp pulled the blanket over the sleeping man. "Good night, me darling Colonel. You are a *good* man. Sleep well."

June 21, 1863

Gum Springs, Va.

The sun poked over the horizon, filling the meadow with its warmth and light of a fresh, new day. The light, poking through the bill of Andrew Ackerman's cap, caused him to stir. *Another warm one,* he thought. Wiping the sleep from his eyes, and slowly rising up, it dawned on him how *quiet* it was. There was none of the *KaaaTHUD!!* of artillery and the muttering crackle of musketry he'd heard on the march of the past few days. The quiet was almost deafening in its silence. *Hmm,* he thought, w*hat is it I'm hearing?* Nothing but birds singing, and the occasional neighing of a horse or two, or possibly the clang of a pot over by where the regimental commissary was.

He stood up, stretched, and looked around to see if anyone else was up. The only one moving was the faithful commissary sergeant who had the camp-fire stirred up and coffee brewing. *Ah yes, good man! Coffee!!* That's *the ticket!* Ackerman half expected a horse with an orderly to come pounding up to the camp with orders to resume the march or to do some picketing. *Nothing. Okay,* he thought, *this* is *interesting.*

A tall, thin man for his day, Ackerman's narrow face came to a thin chin which had a neatly trimmed goatee. His mustache was touched with a bit of gray, which also matched his part. His curly hair came down over the back of his collar. He'd removed his frock coat the night before, so he was in shirt sleeves. He was in his late twenties, but the cares of command and life in general had aged him. He stretched some more, found his boots, and put them on. Pulling his suspenders back over his shoulders, he slowly shuffled over to the camp-fire.

Morning, Cap! was the sergeant's greeting with a quick salute, *and how are you this fine morning, sir?* And before Ackerman could reply, *Coffee, sir?* More of a statement then a question, for he knew exactly what the captain needed. Picking up a tin cup, Ackerman held it out for the other man to pour the hot steaming brew into it. He thought to himself, *Hmmm. That's good, I guess.*

"Thank you, Sergeant!"

"You are more than welcome, sir!"

Ackerman took a sip. *Hmmm! Not bad…And he was* waking up.

He noticed the forms laying around him. The colonel's covered form was curled up under the tree where they had left him the night before. Someone had taken great care to put his kepi over his face just enough to hide his eyes. Ackerman smiled.

The colonel, God knows, really needed this rest, Ackerman reflected. *And he was sleeping the sleep of a dead man.*

A chill ran down Ackerman's spine. *Now where did that come from?* he thought. *The sleep of a dead man.* The chill came again, this time more intense. Must be the morning air. Or was it? He thought about those who were already gone—either killed in combat, or so severely wounded they would never return. A sudden wave of sadness cascaded over him. *I must push these thoughts out of my mind! I have to!*

He was startled out of these thoughts by a warm hand on his shoulder, and a "Now *that* smells like a good cup of coffee!" He turned to see the baby face of Major Philip Kearny and gave a quick nod as a salute. *Oh, one so young,* Ackerman thought. "And how are you this morning, Major?" (Following the resignation of Valentine Mutchler on April 4, 1863, Kearny receives promotion to Major early in May, 1863.)

"Good, Captain! Yourself?"

"Okay…I guess. Oh, the Colonel is sound asleep. Shall we let him sleep a bit more?" McAllister was usually up before anyone, but not this day.

Kearny replied, "Well, there is nothing stirring. Let's let him sleep." The sergeant handed the young major a cup filled with the brew. With his "thank you" barely leaving his lips, he slowly sipped it. *Ummmm very good! And hot too!*

Ackerman stared off at the rising sun. "Well, Major," he said, "how many more of these are in our lot to see??"

Kearny looked at him, a puzzled expression on his face. "Where did *that* thought come from, Ackerman?"

"Oh, just a deep personal sense, a feeling. That one of us, some of us, all of us, may have only a few more days to live. Look, we both know there is a big fight, a very large battle coming. It's going to be on *our* soil this time, but who knows. Who knows? Only God does."

They both sipped the coffee together, and then somewhere in the camp a bugle sounded *Reveille*. The rest of not only the regiment, but the brigade began to stir. The new day had dawned. They both finished their coffee. *Time to wake up the colonel.*

The other men sat up. In twos and threes — some had even just fallen down and gone to sleep where they stood when the regiment halted. So tired they didn't care.

Lieutenant John Faussett woke up. A small, thin man, he was the Second Lieutenant of Company C. As he wiped the sleep from his eyes, he looked around him. Pulling his shoes on, he stood up. Closest to him was a small framed boy. Faussett half chuckled to himself. *Boy, hell, the young boy had become a man now some six weeks ago.* The still sleeping form of one Private Jacob Mount lay not more than five feet away. He noticed the private had fallen asleep, right after they had given the order to fall out. Mount just laid down where he stood. After taking off his pack and laying his rifle down next to him, and placing his hat over his eyes, the young private was fast asleep in moments. Next to him was the form of Mount's good friend, Joseph Cheston (or Joey to all who knew him). *Baby-faced kids both*, thought Faussett. *But veterans now.* Faussett reached over, and poked Mount with his hand.

"Private! Jake, Jacob, wake up!!!"

Typical teenager that he was, Jake just rolled over in his sleep. Again, Faussett poked him, "Come on, Jake; time to get up!" This time, Mount slid his cap from his face and looked up at his officer.

"'Lt.', sir; I am awake, sir! I *am* awake! *Dagnab it!*"

Faussett smiled at him. "Look, son, it's time to get up; you don't want Ackerman over here yelling at you to get going! Do you?"

"I know! I know! I *am* moving!" With that Mount sat up. Of average height and build for the day, he was thin as a rail. His lean frame showed the miles they had marched. His strong hands were already calloused, toughened by the work he had been doing when the war broke out. His blonde hair was matted to his head, and the wisp of a mustache and the three-day growth, the beginnings of a beard, framed his bottom jaw. Deep-set blue eyes, along with a subtle nose, looked perfect for his round face. Before the war, he had a ready smile as one of his now-dead friends noted when they joined up together. But that had been toughened and almost wiped clean by the hell he had seen and lived through at Chancellorsville. As he came more awake, he sighed, stretched, and got up. Putting his shoes on, he forgot to tie them.

Faussett had taken a liking to this young man. Jacob, or Jake to his fellow soldiers, worked hard and had already proven to be steady in combat. He also was a particularly good shot as well. An orphan since the late 1850s, Jake had taken to the lieutenant or "Lt." as he had come to call him. Faussett rustled his hair. "Come on, Jake; it looks like breakfast over at the commissary wagon."

Mount turned to his messmate and poked Cheston in the ribs. Cheston groaned, muttered something to the effect of

"Leave me alone!", and tried to return to sleep.

"Come on, Joey; Faussett woke me up," Mount said, prodding his friend further. "We need to get going."

"All right, all right!" Cheston muttered. "I *am* moving! Dadgum it!"

Cheston had been on a farm in Mercer County, New Jersey, working to help support his widowed mother. Built a lot like Mount but with darker hair, a round face, and deep-set blue eyes. His hands too had been calloused from hard work. Almost the same age as Jake, he had signed up by writing the number eighteen on a piece of paper and putting it into his shoe. So when asked if he was "over eighteen," he could state truthfully he was just that.

The two friends then began their morning ritual of a bit of teasing and a slight bit of horseplay to see who would get to the chow line first.

The rest of the camp continued to stir; Captains William Lloyd and Luther Martin and First Lieutenant William J. Mount also came awake. Finally, the noise of the camp, voices, the smell of coffee and camp-fires, tweaked McAllister's nose! In mid snore, the sound broke off with a snort, and then a sigh. He pulled the hat off his face and slowly sat up. Sgt. Crisp noticed.

"Ahhhh, me darlin' Colonel! You *are* awake! Good, sir! Do you care for a cup of this fine coffee?" Once again the commissary sergeant made more of a statement then a question. McAllister found himself thinking, *How does he always seem to be there when I need something?*

The colonel smiled weakly. "Sergeant, please give me a moment at least to clear my head a bit!" Then, standing before him was Schoonover.

"Colonel, sir; we have orders for the day already. It looks

we are not moving for a while longer." The adjutant handed him the just delivered orders. McAllister quickly scanned them. Then, as he worked out the crick in his neck and the stiffness in his shoulders from sleeping on the hard ground, he sighed in realization that yet *another* quick meeting was necessary.

"Mister Schoonover, please see to it that the officers meet me over under the shade of that cluster of trees over there in about thirty minutes."

Schoonover left and began to move about the camp, contacting the rest of the regiment's officers. Letting them know where to meet and for how long.

Good, McAllister thought to himself, *that gives me a chance to get this bad taste out of my mouth, eat something, and collect my thoughts.* With that, he got up and worked out the kinks in his body. Stretching, trying to loosen the old muscles *still* sore from all the marching, from the miles they had covered. He sighed at the realization of how tired he yet was. *Oh well,* he thought to himself, *it will* have *to do.* He brushed himself off and put on his boots.

Taking a sip of the hot liquid in his tin cup, McAllister took a long look around. The brigade headquarters group was just a short distance from where he stood. He noticed his commander was up and moving about. The rest of the regiments in the brigade were in a circle around the headquarters' cluster of tents. More fires were being lit as the orders for the day reached each of the regimental commanders.

The groomsmen already attended to the officers' horses, making sure they had water and oats. Some of the horses seemed to enjoy the grass of the pasture more than the oats. McAllister found himself chuckling at that thought. He shook his head. It occurred to him there were times when he, too, wished life were *that* simple.

On went his coat and other parts of his uniform. His sword

was where he'd left it the evening before, leaning up against the tree. He made a mental note to not forget where it was. Making his way over to where the quartermaster's and commissary's wagons were located, McAllister took note of the surroundings. The coffee pot hanging over the fire was steaming. The inviting smell of biscuits and of some sort of meat hit his nostrils.

Standing there with plates in hands or pouring coffee were several of the other company officers. Captains John Buckley of Co. A, William P. Dunning of Co. K, Dorastus Logan of Co. H, Luther Martin of Co. D, Thomas Halsey of Co. E, William H. Lloyd of Co. F, John Meyer of Co. G, and Surgeon Edward Welling. Lt. John Sowter of Co. B, filling in for his commander Captain William Meeker out on sick leave, also was there. All present greeted their colonel with crisp salutes and good mornings to him in the most heartfelt manner.

All of these men were of roughly the same size and bearing. Buckley — a quiet man who listened more and led by quiet example. Dunning — more outgoing, loved to discuss the issues of the day. Logan — another quiet yet solid officer, though a bit of a disciplinarian. Martin — could be gregarious to a fault. Lloyd — more of the studious type, but brave, in some cases brave to a fault. And then Welling — a solid surgeon who knew his job and was honing his craft.

Major Kearny did double duty ever since Lt. Colonel Stephen Moore was in hospital still suffering from the aftereffects of heatstroke. It was hoped Moore could shortly return. Until then Kearny had to do *two* jobs: the duties Moore normally would handle, plus his own. For a young officer who was still learning on the job, it could be overwhelming at times.

From the back of the commissary wagon, Sergeant Crisp handed McAllister a tin plate filled with a biscuit, bacon, and grits. Smiling, he said, "Here you go, Colonel, sir! Enjoy!" The other officers had already tended to themselves. The regiment's enlisted men had fires going to brew up coffee and cook some meat or whatever they had scrounged for. McAllister sat down on a log next to Lt. Mount, who munched on a biscuit. Mount had been promoted from Sergeant Major about two months prior.

"Good morning, Lieutenant; how are you this fine morning?"

Mount looked up, with a quizzical look on his face. "I, err, am…um, doing well Colonel; doing well!"

"Lieutenant, I wanted to take a moment and thank you for the thorough job you did in the recent inventory of our supplies. Well done, sir; well done!"

Mount, who was known to be a quiet sort, looked into the face of his colonel. "Why, thank you, sir! That means a great deal! Sir, a question if I may?"

"What's on your mind?"

Mount took a deep breath and sighed. "Begging the Colonel's pardon! Is it possible that well, in the fight that *is* coming, I can assist Surgeon Welling?"

As Mount bowed his head and looked at the ground, McAllister replied. "Lieutenant, you did so well at Chancellorsville! You held your company in line, kept them from running! In all that deadly confusion and chaos, you showed *great* courage!"

Mount continued staring at the ground, pursing his lips, his face going pale.

"What is it, mister? What has you so worked up? Look at me, son!"

Mount's head snapped upright. Had he heard his colonel right? *"Look at me, son!"* There it was again! Mount sat up straight.

"Come and walk with me for a moment," McAllister said. And they got up together. They moved a short distance to a spot where he thought they were out of hearing of everyone else.

"William," he said, as he looked into the eyes of the younger officer, "every man knows fear in a fight! *Even I do!*" Mount smiled at that thought; everyone in the regiment was *sure* the colonel was fearless. "Look, son, we are going to need every man to do his duty! *Every* officer to show courage in this fight that's coming! We must all hold ourselves together! Most importantly, trust in God. *He* will see you through!"

Mount blinked several times, trying to grasp the fact that his colonel, a man who could very well be his father, had just called him "son." A term he had never heard used by the colonel in all the time he had known him! He looked into McAllister's eyes, shocked surprise plainly evident on his face.

"Colonel, sir, thank you," Mount stammered out. "Thank you for your patience with me! Thank you for calling me 'son'! I deeply appreciate it. Deeply. More than you ever know. I will not let you down, sir!"

Mount looked down to see McAllister's extended hand, offering a handshake. Mount took it, but McAllister covered it with his other hand. Looking Mount straight in the eye, he said, "William, I know you will not fail. I know the regiment, *the men*, and I know I *can* depend on you! Now, let us see to this rest of this day!"

Mount turned back to the wagon to gather up the rest of his belongings. McAllister turned toward all the other officers gathered there for the morning meeting. In doing so, he noticed many of them stood there. They looked at the ground, at the trees on the edge of the pasture, and in every other direction—but not at him.

Schoonover's look told him the story. They had all heard the conversation, or parts of it, that had just taken place. Some had approving looks, some gave smirks; most wore this look of bafflement. Here their colonel, this martinet, this man of cold steeliness, had just done something so totally out of character from what they knew of him before today. Well, they *now* saw him in a completely different light! In Schoonover's hand were the orders for the day. The piece of paper hung limply in the humid morning air, like it was the least important thing in the world. For that conversation had changed everything. The use of *Mother McAllister* now took on a whole different level of meaning. He actually did care for them. All of them....

Still aboard the train...

Schoonover awoke with a snort, mid snore. His wife looked at him. "John, you have been dreaming and talking in your sleep." She smiled. "You've been dreaming about the regiment again, haven't you?"

He smiled, sitting up right with the soothing *clickety clack* droning sound that trains make as they go forward. "Yes, my dear, I have. They are all on my mind. How could they not be?"

Back to the speech, he thought. He again pulled out the rough draft he'd been working on. That dream which seemed so real kept coming back into his mind. Struggling to focus on it all, the words *he cared for all of us,* running through his mind. He shook his head, and went back to reading what he'd previously written....

June 22, 1863
Gum Springs, Va.

The previous day ended with some light drill, the men in the ranks cleaning weapons, getting rid of the Virginia dust that worked its way into the barrels and into the firing mechanisms of the guns.

The Eleventh was equipped with four different types of muskets; three of them were rifled. One company, however, still had the smoothbore musket originally issued them. A .69 calibre beast that kicked like a mule. This musket was preferred by quite a few Union regiments, for it was deadly at close distances. The typical round was a buck and ball type. That meant a large .69 calibre ball with three other .44 caliber or smaller rounds of buckshot with it. When fired, the buck and ball round spread out like a shotgun, capable of causing devastating damage to its target. Its biggest drawback lay in not being accurate past fifty to seventy-five yards. Another drawback lay in its recoil. It could recoil so badly that the musket's muzzle lifted and caused its user to miss his target.

The other muskets were a .57 calibre Springfield Rifle Musket, a .58 Trenton Springfield Contract Rifled Musket, and then finally a monster .72 rifled Belgian musket. McAllister had been working since Chancellorsville to get rid of both this behemoth and the .69 calibre smoothbore. The problem was there *still* weren't enough guns to go around. The regiment had replaced a number of guns during Chancellorsville by simply picking up what was left on the ground after the battle.

McAllister and his officers met twice this day to go over the state of the regiment. After the first one, McAllister asked Schoonover to briefly remain behind. "Mr. Schoonover, we need to review our leadership makeup. We really haven't had time to do so since Chancellorsville. Our loss was so heavy, especially among the lieutenants and the sergeants. We need to settle that issue. What was our total casualty count from that battle?"

"One-hundred-and-eighty-five, sir," Schoonover replied.

McAllister sighed. "I almost forgot our loss; and yes, it was so great. We lost so many fine officers and men…." They both fell silent for what to John seemed hours. McAllister continued, "Lieutenants Bloomfield and Kelly of Co. B, as well as Sergeants Cox of Co. A, McDavitt of Co. E, and Bender of Co. H were all such good, *good* men. Not to mention the corporals and privates we lost. It's a shame they had to fall." The emotion that hung on the air was heavy on both.

"Well, we must not dwell on it," McAllister said, finally. "We must re-focus ourselves to the task before us. So, Lieutenant, let us see to do this."

Around them as they bent over the rosters of each company, camp life continued. Letter writing home to wives and sweethearts and noting comments in personal diaries were the main duties of the day. Even some time for a baseball game between the Eleventh New Jersey and the Twelfth New Hampshire. No score was kept, but a good time had by all. The other was back to usual practice; the day began with prayer. With the retirement of the previous chaplain and waiting on a new one, the Twelfth New Hampshire and the Fifth New Jersey chaplains led services. Which by this time, were well attended, as the men had well "learned" it was a good idea to do so. The chaplain of the Twelfth New Hampshire delivered a sermon from the Letter to the Philippians, chapter three. Its title? "Press On!" There were also camp-fires, so they were constantly tended to. Coffee was always brewing. *Always.*

The day wore on. More cleaning of uniforms and weapons. Someone found a stream nearby and all who could, stripped down and jumped in. To wash the grime and grit off that had accumulated.

McAllister was in his tent, writing orders when John Schoonover approached with the commissary sergeant in tow. "Colonel, sir!"

Sgt. Major Tilton was leaning up against a tent post. He had been promoted to his position with Mount receiving his officer's commission back in April, 1863. Another young man at age twenty-three, his boyish looks made him appear a lot younger than he was. He stood up straight and saluted Schoonover as the latter approached.

"Yes, Adjutant," McAllister responded.

"Commissary Sergeant Crisp here, sir, informs me we are low on supplies. He recommends we acquire some! From the locals, sir; being we are in 'secesh' country. Help to donate to the 'right side' of the cause." Both Crisp and Schoonover had slight smirks on their faces.

"You are at attention, sirs! Wipe the smirks off your faces!" McAllister rapped out. "Oh, all right…" Grabbing a piece of paper and dipping a pen into an inkwell, he quickly scrawled a few lines. "Lieutenant, you have an order here to put a detail together and well, go requisition some supplies. Make sure you have a sizable contingent with you. And take a wagon! Right, Sgt. Crisp?"

"Yes, sir!" Crisp replied. "We shall do our best!"

McAllister just shook his head from side to side. "See to it, you two. Now, get going! I have more work to do!"

As the two turned to leave, McAllister said, "Lt. Schoonover, are your duties as adjutant complete? Updated rosters and sick reports? Day Book also?"

"Yes, sir!" Schoonover replied.

"Well, then get going."

Both men snapped a salute, and with a "By your leave sir," left the colonel's tent. With Crisp in tow, John headed over to Company A, to get some men for the expedition. Instead, they ran into Privates Cheston and Mount.

"Privates," Schoonover asked the pair, "are you busy?"

"Why do you ask, sir?" Jake responded.

"Well, we have been ordered to go requisition some supplies."

"That's all?" Joe Cheston said.

"Well, it's from the locals," Crisp replied.

Mount looked at his dear friend. With an excited look on his face, Jake said, "Then, let's go with them!!"

"Why not," Cheston responded. "Sounds like a great adventure. Beats sitting around here all day!"

Crisp had already procured a wagon and a team to drive it. Before they all knew it, their little group had grown to ten men as word spread around the regiment of the foraging party.

"Men," Schoonover said, "gather round. We have been ordered to go requisition some supplies from the locals. Keep in mind, men; we are in 'secesh' territory and need to be alert! Be sure to grab your accoutrements and rifles! Check your cartridge boxes and cap boxes to make sure you've sufficient ammunition!"

Within moments, the entire party reassembled. Schoonover ordered them to fall in as a column of twos, and at the right shoulder shift. With his little band in tow, he went out the gate and onto the road. He headed north, looking for a farm not already "visited" by troops from the Third Corps. On their own, the men went from right shoulder shift to more of a carry arms, holding their guns across their chests or loosely pointing ahead of them, fingers on triggers. It was a beautiful day for this little lark, and they enjoyed every moment. A few of them made sure to turn around and look behind them so they did not get surprised.

Finally, a farmhouse came into view. Nicely kept, and a barn looking a bit careworn. No sign of humans other than the door to the barn was open. There were a couple of cows in a pasture behind the barn.

Schoonover led this little band into the yard and began looking around. "Mount, Cheston," he said, "take a couple of the other men and check the corn shed and smoke house. You other men, help Crisp load as much provisions as you can. You two," pointing to two other men who seemed reluctant to do anything, "you can be guards or lookouts. Keep a keen eye! Remember the report from some of the other regiments that found men who hadn't returned hung from a tree."

Along with the other men with them, Jake and Joe found the corn shed stuffed to the rafters with good feed for men and animals alike. The smoke house was filled with all kinds of meats. All cured and ready to eat. That was cleaned out in a hurry. The others pulled the cows in and tied them to the back of the wagon. Quickly they gathered their newfound supplies and began to leave.

A shotgun suddenly appeared out of an upstairs window of the farmhouse. An angry voice yelled, "You d____yankee bluebellies!!! Now that y'all have stripped us clean, y'all better high tail it out of here!" For emphasis, the farmer fired both barrels in rapid succession, missing Schoonover's head by inches. The buckshot whistled past everyone else. Schoonover turned, doffed his hat in a mock bow, and spurred his horse. Crisp thought about a "giddy-yap" to the team with the wagon. But with the two cows tied to it, he was not about to go anywhere real fast. The others leveled their muskets at the window, ready to shoot.

"Let him be," Schoonover ordered. "We did more harm to him by taking his cows and supplies."

The wagon lurched and bounced as it left the yard. The men started hooting and hollering, as they jumped up on the back of the wagon.

"Hey there, old Reb," Mount yelled, "we got you for all you're worth, secesh!"

"D____ *you, you yella bluebellies!*" The shotgun roared again, kicking up the dirt around them.

"Thanks for the supplies, you grayback!!!" Cheston yelled.

And shortly they were out of range. They could still hear the angry imprecations of the farmer as they crested the nearby hill and were out of sight. They sat in the back of the wagon as it bucked and bumped along on the return journey. Some of the party carefully walked along, with rifles at the ready and watching for any potential ambush. One of the men had a harmonica, so he started playing *Frog in the Well, Battle Cry of Freedom*, and even *Hail Columbia*. A couple of them kept looking out the back of the wagon to make sure no one was following.

"Maybe the Rebs are so busy trying to get into Pennsylvania," Cheston said, "they have forgot, or they don't know about us!" They all chuckled at the witty remark.

Led by Schoonover, it wasn't long before they turned back into the pasture and pulled right up in front of McAllister and the other tents. Curious as to the entourage, nearly everyone in the regiment ambled over. Especially since it was the center of where everything was, particularly the camp-fires for cooking.

McAllister stepped out of his tent; drawn from it to see what all the commotion was. "Schoonover," he said, "I see you were successful! No issues I pray?"

"Ohhhh, nothing that got us into any real trouble," Schoon-over responded.

Jake spoke up from the back of the wagon. "Well, Colonel, except for these holes on the cover over the wagon from the shotgun blasts! Wow! Just missed us!" Schoonover had this look on his face. *Oh, Mount, why did you have to say that!* But either McAllister didn't hear it or chose to ignore it, as he didn't react at all to Mount's comments.

They all dismounted, flipped the tailgate down, and began the unloading of the collected supplies. The cows were led off to be tied to a tree for milk and most likely dinner down the road. After that was all done, Schoonover reported to McAllister with what had gone on. That done, with a salute and "with your permission, sir," Schoonover returned to his tent. Sgt. Crisp lit the fires for dinner and started to get the evening meal ready. Jake and Joe returned to their little corner of the war so to speak. To write letters home or reread for the hundredth time the letters they had received. The other men who had made up the party did much the same.

Eventually the sun began to set on this day, and all gathered at the commissary wagon for meals or cooked whatever they had on them over a local fire. Lights out was sounded and the day was done.

June 25, 1863
Gum Springs, Va.

Schoonover awoke to the sounds of his own snoring. He rubbed his eyes and stretched on his cot. They had only gotten their tents yesterday as the regimental wagons had finally caught up with them.

The stirrings of camp caught his attention. Once again he briefly panicked — just like the last day at their camp of instruction. But this time, he found he was so weary. *Well,* he thought, *after the events of yesterday, the colonel would understand.* He swung his feet over the side and stretched again. He tossed the tent flap aside to see to the day. *Reveille* had not yet sounded, but camp was already getting into the course of the day. After quickly dressing, he stepped out of his tent. He noticed they were now surrounded by all of the officers' tents of the other five regiments in the brigade. Their overall commander, Brigadier General Joseph Carr, had his own headquarters in the middle. Even there they were stirring. Flags now began to stir in the warm summer breezes. *Thank God for that,* Schoonover thought to himself.

Not too far away, on his company street, Pvt. Jacob Mount's shelter tent had been constructed and set up. One half being his and the other his pal Joe Cheston. Jake was a little bit older than Joe, but they had grown close as the war had dragged on. Cheston had proven to be a crack shot. Although not an orphan like Jake, Joe found they shared a lot in common. Hard working young men from farming towns in central New Jersey. Both had answered the call at the same time.

They and two others were now all that were left under the age of eighteen from those who had initially joined up with the Eleventh for a number of reasons. Adventure, patriotism, impress a girl. Both had girls back home. And they shared their letters with each other. With tears in his eyes, Joe looked up from re-reading the latest letter from his girl. He read Jake a few lines from it. *Oh, my dearest Joseph, oh to see you again, to hold you close, to feel your muscles, the depths of your love for me that pour from your eyes. Oh, I long to be there again.*

"Jake," he said in a low tone, "how do I get back to her? How do I return to this woman, the love of my life? How?" He pulled the letter close to his chest. "Ooh my dearest Beverly, oh my love…" Cheston wiped the tears from his eyes, blew his nose.

Jake pulled out his girl's last letter from his haversack. Sara Jean wrote such incredibly passionate letters, filled with a longing for him. This time she had included a lock of her hair. And oh, that perfume!!! Every sniff of it overwhelmed him with a longing to see her. *That's not going to be for a long time,* he thought. Jake put down his letter, and sighed.

Joe looked at him. "What's the matter? Missin' your girl?" A look of deep sadness, the look that can age anyone in seconds, came over Jake's face. "Well *that,* and another thing…"

"Oh, yeah?" Cheston asked.

In a sad tone, Jake said, "I miss Billy Fraley."

"Crazy, happy-go-lucky Billy?" Cheston said. "Who loved to pull little practical jokes, who thought our soldiering was a total lark, who laughed at all our lame attempts at humor, and all of that stuff?"

"Yeah," Jake replied. "We lost him at Chancellorsville. Don't you remember?" Cheston nodded in recollection. "He was supporting the sharp-shooters there, when he was severely wounded. He died a couple days later."

Continuing, Jake said, "To be well, ya know, open about it…that was the first time I *really* was confronted with my own frail humanity! You know as well as I do, that a soldier's life is mostly complete utter boredom punctuated with episodes of heart-pounding, absolute fear!"

Warming to the grim topic, Jake went on. "We live from day to day; take for instance, what happened yesterday! One moment we are laying around reading letters or newspapers from home, or brewing coffee, or just talking about anything, and within minutes, shotgun pellets are whistling around our heads! But for an inch here or half an inch there, one of us, *all of us* are either dead or even badly wounded. How does one even as young as we are come to grips with that? Think about it, Joe! Most guys at our age are back on the farm or thinking about whatever needs doing to move on with life. Why, back home right now, we'd be thinking about being with our favorite girls and getting ready to settle down. All we can do now, is hope and pray we get to live out the rest of our days...."

Mouth agape, Joe just looked at his friend, incredulous at what he'd just heard. "Really? Is that what you are so caught up in? Haven't you been listening to the chaplains, or even to *Mother McAllister* when he talks about trusting in God?"

Jake just nodded, unable to really reply. Joe continued, reinforcing the point. "Don't you believe in divine providence? Where is your faith in God?"

Pulling in his lower lip for a moment, Jake said, "Yeah, I 'spose you're right. But, still...." His voice trailed off. The sudden squawk of a bugle call snapped him out of his reverie. "Somethin' up," he muttered.

Cheston could only reply, "Yep."

A rider on a dark brown horse, with the tail straight out, came pounding up to the group of tents where their brigade commander was. The order was given to an aide, who signed a receipt for it and then, with a salute handed it to the mutton-chopped and mustachioed general. The next sound was a bugle call, for *Officer's Call* to Carr's tent. With that all the commanding officers of the regiments in the brigade headed toward it. McAllister, as well as Kearny and Schoonover, did so as well. In only moments, the leaders all returned to their regiments, and the Long Roll sounded.

Cheston and Mount looked at each other. They both knew what this all meant. They would be moving out again. The long respite, the break, was *over*. They scrambled together, knocking their tent down, briskly wiping off whatever ground clutter had clung to it. Then they took their gum blanket ground covers, placed their folded blankets in them, as well as each half of their shelter tent, and rolled them up together. (Both had found that this bedroll was best carried over the left shoulder tied to the right side of the waist.) They put their haversacks on their left hip first, and their cartridge box with sling on their right hip. Equipment belt with cap box and bayonet in scabbard then went on. Next the completed bedroll was put on, with the canteen over it for easier access. Checking each other just as all the other tent mates were doing, they quickly completed the breakdown of their little home for the last four days. Then the bugle call to fall in by company was sounded and quickly done. All the men took their usual positions in their companies, forming two rows.

The roll was taken, the first sergeant of each company reporting to the senior lieutenant of each. That lieutenant then reported to his captain that all were indeed present and accounted for. McAllister and Kearny had mounted their horses and sat on them in front of the regiment. Schoonover also was on his horse near the colonel.

Around them, all the other regiments in the brigade were going through the same process. Of course, the commissary had more to do. Knock down fires and pack up. All the commissary wagons, however, would follow behind the brigade with the rest of the brigade wagon trains.

As each regiment finished falling in, its adjutant made report to brigade headquarters to the brigade adjutant. This was so General Carr would know each of his regiments was ready. A cluster of men sat up on a slight rise observing the whole scene. The guidon told them all it was their division commander, Brigadier General Andrew A. Humphreys, who was present. This was a serious moment. It was going to be all business now.

The band formed up and began to play martial music. They started off with "Frog in the Well." With that Carr nodded, and the Eleventh made the move to lead off. Already formed into a column of fours, the regiment began moving. *By the right wheel, forward, march!* With McAllister in the lead and colors also unfurled, the regiment, the brigade, and the rest of the entire Third Corps behind them resumed the long march at ten A.M.

To whatever fate awaited.

Chapter Three
ECHOES OF BATTLE

June 29, 1863 5 P.M.

Just north of Taneytown, Maryland

BRIGADIER GENERAL Joseph Carr raised his hand to indicate
Column, halt! The whole brigade column came to an accordion-like
stop. "Pass the word," Carr said to his own adjutant, "this is a ten-
minute halt."

At the head of his own regimental column was McAllister.
"Order, Arms! Parade, rest." All in a row from the colonel. "Fall out
men, get off your feet, and drink some water."

The men slowly went to a grove on the side of the road, to find
shelter under some trees in an orchard. They soon noticed a cloud
of dust from the direction of Taneytown, the town they'd passed
through only a few hours ago. That dust cloud indicated riders coming in.

Slowly, but steadily, a flag came into view. *What unit is this? Oh,
the flag is a corps flag.* The group of soldiers came into view. And as
it did, there was at first a murmur, *who was it?* It grew to cheers from
the ranks as Major General Daniel E. Sickles, commander of their
own Third Corps of the Army of the Potomac, and staff came into
view. The sound continued to grow. *"It's General Sickles!!" "It's old*

53

Dan!" The sound of huzzahs and even wild passionate cheering escalated. The further Sickles and his party rode into where the corps had stopped, the cheering rolled over it. The men came running up to the road. Forgetting their sore feet and their tiredness, they cheered him with everything they had and swung their caps lustily from side to side.

Schoonover and McAllister found themselves caught up in this. *His men adore him,* Schoonover noted to himself. Sickles, *the greatest general in the army* as far as they all were concerned, was back with the old Third Corps. With divisional commander General Humphreys out reconnoitering, it was up to Carr to welcome this group of officers. After saluting, he shook Sickles's hand.

Sickles was a short, wiry man, with a full round face, and a full mustache that came down around his mouth. His past was one of a hard living, hard drinking, and hard loving man. His entire claim to fame was he was a Congressman from New York before the war and had raised a whole brigade from that state. Also before the war, he pleaded temporary insanity after he shot and killed his wife's lover, none other than the son of Francis Scott Key.

"Welcome, sirs! General Sickles, sir, welcome back! I am sure you want to see the division?"

"Well, General Carr," Sickles replied, "I am not sure we will have time. Would you have the officers of the division meet with me, along with the other division and brigade commanders, over in that grove? Say, in five minutes?"

Sickles went back to his horse and pulled out a couple of cigars. Giving them a sniff, he then turned to the grove. Once there, Generals David Birney (acting commander of the Third Corps in Sickles's absence), Carr, Charles Graham, and Colonel George Burling of the Second New Jersey brigade joined him. All the regimental colonels of Humphreys's division, including McAllister with Kearny and Schoonover, were with Carr.

"Gentlemen," Sickles started speaking, "we are going to stay here for a while to let the quartermasters catch up with us with their trains as the majority of the men are either barefoot or almost so. A supply of shoes will be arriving shortly, most likely by night-fall."

One of his aides pulled out a map and unrolled it on a small table that had been set up. "We are here," Sickles said, pointing to a spot just north of Taneytown. "After the issuance of shoes, we will march back through Taneytown. We will then proceed from there up through Emmitsburg, Maryland."

Continuing further, puffing on one of the cigars he'd lit, he noted, "I am awaiting orders from the General Commanding the army who, by the way, has changed. 'Fighting Joe' Hooker no longer leads our valiant army of the Republic." His face for a brief moment roiled into almost a scowl. "Major General George Meade, late of the Fifth Corps, now commands."

"We are headed most likely into southern Pennsylvania as the rebel army is gathering towards the Chambersburg, Cashtown, Get-tysburg area." He showed on the map where it was thought the Army of Northern Virginia was concentrating. "We are going to spend the night here," pointing on the map, "in Taneytown or this general area. So our supplies can catch up to us. As soon as the shoes arrive, you will have them. Generals Birney and Graham, and you too, Colonel Burling…once your commands approach closer to the area of the town, have your men fall out, and rest for the night. In General Humphreys's absence, General Carr, have your brigade en-camp here. Again, have your men rest easy. Any questions? If not, you are all dismissed. Return to your units."

All the officers assembled saluted Sickles and moved back to-ward their brigades and regiments. As he returned to the Eleventh, with Kearny and Schoonover in town, McAllister said, "Well, this is going to be good news to the men. I know so many are without footwear." Kearny nodded his head in agreement.

Turning to Kearny, he said, "Major, please have the regiment fall in. We need to keep the men informed."

With that, Kearny bellowed, "*Attention, Battalion! Fall in…*" At that order, the men who had moments before given their beloved corps commander a heartfelt welcome back, and started fires for coffee, resumed all their places in line. The young Major then called out, *"Battalion, Attentttionnn!!!"*

McAllister followed that with, "At rest, men. I have an announcement to make. We are going to spend the night here, so our supply trains can catch up to us. They have what I am sure so many of you need so desperately, shoes and socks! We will let you know, and we will call you when the wagons arrive. You are dismissed," McAllister said, grinning, "to return to your coffee."

With dismissal, the regiment headed back to the coffee boilers and the camp-fires for the night.

June 30, 1863
Morning, Still just north of Taneytown, Maryland

Reveille sounded, almost too loud. Another day, a new day, had dawned. The men who basically had gone to sleep on the hard ground all began to stir. With the divisions so close together, it did not take long for all the men to get up, to make coffee again and munch on their hard army bread. Schoonover, who had been up since sunrise, noted all of this around him. He also saw how many of the residents of the surrounding area came into the camps, to satisfy their curiosity at never having seen an army on the march. Then, in the far distance, another dust cloud seemed to rise out of the road, or the ground itself.

Schoonover muttered to himself, "The supply trains are coming. *The supply trains are coming!!!*" As it rang through his head, he tossed away his coffee and went running to McAllister's location.

McAllister, who was up already, stood up from his bench in front of his travel desk, where he had continued a letter to home. To Schoonover, he said, "Easy, Lieutenant, go ahead and alert the regiment. Tell the company commanders to have their men fall in…"

Being what they were, leaf spring with wooden wheels and iron tires, the wagons eventually drew up with a creak and a clatter in front of the brigade. Other wagons did the same thing with all the other brigades of the Corps. Strung out in a long line, one could tell they were weighted down.

Schoonover had the bugler sound the "Fall in." In an instant it seemed as if they were all anticipating this moment. *"Attention, Battalion!"* Schoonover announced when the men were assembled. *"Fall out, by company, for issuance of shoes and stockings."*

A smile creased his face as well as all the officers'. Even they knew, they would perhaps need some new footwear. As much as everyone needed shoes, it was orderly. When called, each man stepped up and received his allotment of new shoes and new socks.

Mount and Cheston were together as they were handed their new shoes and socks. After leaving the company line, Jake held up his. "Um, Joe, I think mine are a bit too small for me. What about yours?"

Cheston took a closer look as well at his. "I think mine are way too big for me!"

Jake replied, "Want to swap?"

"Sure!" Joe replied. Within seconds they were trying on their new shoes. Both stood up and tested them out. They grinned broadly at each other; a perfect fit!

When the supplies of new shoes and clothing were all issued, there was another bugle call for the assembly and the order to fall in. It wasn't long before the order to march came. With that, they set off to resume their journey northwards. To whatever lay ahead.

Sickles was with his staff on a porch of a local tavern in Taneytown as they went by. As his men passed him, he tipped his hat rather than saluting, as another wave of huzzahs and lusty cheers rolled out.

Close to Emmitsburg Md.
July 1, 1863

They marched northward for about four miles and another halt was called. Entering an already harvested wheatfield, the regiment received orders to camp there for the night. When *Reveille* sounded the next morning, most of the corps was up and making coffee.

Sgt. Major Tilton cleverly found a way to boil coffee for himself, the colonel, and the regimental staff, including Kearny and Schoonover. McAllister was awake as well. The ground was not really suitable for sleeping, so it had been a restless night for him. The three senior members of the regiment approached the camp-fire together, as the smell of the boiling coffee alerted them to their need.

A rider pounded into their bivouac, and handed Schoonover an order. This one came from the new commanding general, Major General George Gordon Meade. Schoonover showed it to McAllister, who nodded his head as he sipped his coffee.

"Mr. Schoonover," McAllister said, "please call the regiment to form a square, say, over there."

"Attention, Battalion!" Schoonover yelled. *"Form square, on me, now!"*

There were muffled groans of weariness, or grunts, as this tired band of less than 300 got to their collective feet. Within moments, a square had formed up with McAllister, Schoonover, and Kearny in the middle.

Stepping forward, Schoonover cleared his throat. When he saw everyone was ready and attentively listening, he continued:

"Headquarters, Army of the Potomac, June 30th, 1863.

"The Commanding General requests that previous to the engagement soon expected with the enemy, corps and all other commanding officers will address their troops, explaining to them briefly the immense issues involved in this struggle. The enemy are on our soil; the whole country now looks anxiously to the army to deliver it from the presence of the foe. Our failure to do so will leave us no such welcome as the swelling of millions of hearts with pride and joy at our success would give to every soldier in the army. Homes, friends, and domestic altars are involved. The army has fought well heretofore; it is believed that it will fight more desperately and bravely than ever if it is addressed in fitting terms. Corps and other commanders are authorized to order the instant death of any soldier who fails in his duty at this hour.

"By command of Major-General Meade.

"S. Williams, A. A. G."[1]

Schoonover stepped back. Then it was McAllister's turn. In a passionate tone that was unusual even for him, he lifted his deep baritone voice and addressed the assembled regiment.

"Sons of New Jersey, the hour of battle is at hand. The soil of Pennsylvania is the contested field. We *must* stand shoulder-to-shoulder with her sons and drive the enemy from her borders, cost what it may. Your past bright record is a guarantee to me that you will not falter. In the dark days of the Revolution, when the gallant Jersey Blues were fighting for liberty upon their own soil, their Pennsylvania brothers rushed to their assistance and helped them triumph. We are now called upon to do for Pennsylvania what she did for us. Now with hearts filled with love of country and a firm reliance on God, let us go forward. Are you ready for the march and the fight?"[2]

What happened next was something that all in attendance would never forget. These tired, foot-sore soldiers, who had been hanging on every word of their colonel, broke spontaneously into three rousing cheers of *"Yes! Yes! Yes!"* Caught up in the moment, Schoonover emotionally called for a loud *Huzzah!,* which was then resoundingly given three times. At that, McAllister ordered the regiment to reform for the march, and back onto it they went.

The column reached Emmitsburg at about noon, and found the

---

[1] Marbaker, Thomas E. *History of the Eleventh New Jersey Volunteers: From its Organization to Appomattox: to Which is Added Experiences of Prison Life and Sketches of Individual Members.* MacCrellish & Quigley, book and job printers, Trenton, New Jersey; 1898. Reprinted 1991 by Longstreet House, Hightstown, New Jersey; page 91.

[2] *Ibid.,* pp. 92–93.

town partially destroyed by fire. A rumor spread quickly through the ranks that a pro-Southern sympathizer was responsible. Kearny was heard muttering, "those d_____ Copperheads!" Following a short halt just beyond the town, the regiment pressed on. It wasn't long thereafter they crossed the Mason and Dixon's line into Pennsylvania. Once more on the soil of a Northern state, the men were greeted by a German woman who came out of her house. Holding a pail of water, she said, "Here's Pennsylvania water for you boys!" All took advantage of the proffered refreshment and thanked the woman with three hearty cheers for the old Keystone state. Up ahead they heard the echoes of the muttering crackle of musketry and the booming of cannon. The men in the ranks held their rifles a little tighter; although tired, their step now had a slight spring, a slight urgency to it. The "ball" was about to be joined; the enemy had at last been found. Destiny awaited.

Near Midnight, July 1/2, 1863
On a road toward Gettysburg

They had been marching most of the night. The full moon, which had been slowly rising for most of the march, hung over them. The moon dissipated what had begun as one of the darkest nights in memory, turning it into a soft, well-lit landscape. The Eleventh pushed on, acutely aware of the need to rejoin the rest of the army. In the lead of his regimental column, McAllister alternated between riding and walking with his men. To try and keep himself awake, he went back and forth between prayer, humming hymns, and running other things through his mind. Memories at times of home, and hearth, of hugs from his wife. Just *anything* to stay awake, to cope with the exhaustion that pressed in. The only other thing keeping him awake were the footfalls of thousands of pairs of feet. Pounding on…pushing on through the night. Kearny, Schoonover, Ackerman,

Mount, all the company commanders, kept prodding the men. Sometimes with a hushed *"Close up, men; press on!"*, or if they had to, the flat of the blade of their sword, to keep soldiers from turning into stragglers. From giving into the fatigue that now gripped them all. More hushed tones of encouragement, *"Come on, men. Press on. Press on."*

Schoonover slowly gained on his colonel. "Colonel, sir; are you all right, sir?"

McAllister looked up; a weary smile crossed his face. "Tired, but we *must* press on. There has been serious fighting up ahead this past day." He pulled out his pocket watch. By the light of the brightly shining full moon, he stole a quick glance. *By the Almighty, McAllister thought, it's almost midnight! We have been at this now for how long?* The minutes seemed like hours; the hours seemed like an eternity. Once again, the word passed down the column. "Press on. Press on. *Press on.*"

Up ahead, Brigadier General A. A. Humphreys sat ramrod straight in his saddle. The division guidon hung limp in the damp, warm night air. Someone had gotten a guide or a farmer or someone who knew the ground; the guide was leading the column. With the Eleventh New Jersey the leading regiment of both the brigade and the division, McAllister heard the discussion ahead between Humphreys, Carr, Brewster, Burling, and the guide.

Then, abruptly, the call came for the column to halt. They were at a place where another road came in from the left. There was animated discussion, with much gesturing. The guide insisted they must make a left turn onto the new road; the others equally insisted they should go straight ahead. The column made the left turn. After a few miles, another sudden halt occurred.

Carr came back ever so slowly, his horse's hooves barely making a sound on the road. "Colonel McAllister," he whispered.

"Yes, sir," was the as softly whispered reply.

"Pick some of your best men," Carr said. "Leave your colors here and follow me."

"Pass the word," McAllister said quietly to Schoonover. "I need Kearny here *now!*" Whispers back along the column quickly caught up with Kearny. It was only a moment before he was next to the colonel. "Yes, sir. What are your orders?"

"Kearny, please have the first platoon of Company A load quietly," McAllister replied. "Have them leave behind canteens and anything else that will clank or make noise. Then, have them come with me. Also, before you give the order to Company A, make sure the color guard covers the flags. The last thing we need is to have them get caught in a breeze and snap out!"

Kearny quietly called to Captain Buckley of Company A: "Captain, give me the first platoon from your company. You heard the Colonel; pass along those orders."

In response, Buckley quickly located Mount and passed on the orders. "Mr. Mount. First platoon with us. You heard the Colonel."

Again, only a moment passed. When the first platoon of Co. A reached McAllister, he said: "Men, quietly follow me along with Buckley, Schoonover, and Mount." To Kearny, the colonel whispered, "Kearny, you are in charge. If there is any firing of any kind, put the regiment into battle line and block the road. We may need a rear guard if this goes bad."

The men moved out with Humphreys, Carr, Brewster, Burling, and their staffs in the lead. The moon, which had played peek-a-boo with them throughout their march, illumined the road ahead. They crept forward; their collective tired bodies now twitched with every nerve on edge as they stepped. Every sense was now fully alert as the adrenaline accented every nerve, every fiber. All had a grim look of determination. All the enlisted men were ready to bring their weapons into a firing position if needed. The officers up ahead dismounted quietly and walked forward, the guide now in the lead. Suddenly hands went up, stopping the small column in its tracks. Tension hung in the air; time seemed to stop; hearts pounded in McAllister and his men.

Then the escorts and the generals came hurriedly back, with men in blindfolds and rope-bound hands behind their backs, shuffling by the colonel. Back to where he had left McAllister and the others, Carr leaned into where McAllister stood. In a whisper, he said, "*That* was close, Colonel; we almost marched into the Rebel's lines! Thank goodness a nearby farmer told us the Reb has a battery commanding the road just a short distance ahead!"

Hearing that, Schoonover thought to himself, *Oh, that would have been great! We bring on a fight but at night! And no one nearby to help us!*

Seething with anger, Humphreys stopped next to McAllister and Carr. "Listen, men; I am ordering an about face of the entire column. We need to turn around and go back from whence we came, and then bear left at the road we originally were on. Our own army is up that original road a bit. Not too far, a couple of miles; we are just about there." He sighed, exhaling his frustration with the guide. "At least we didn't bring on a fight. It was close. *Too d___ ______ close.* It was all I could do to *not* shoot the guide myself! But that would have alerted the enemy's videttes."

"Sir? Am I right?" McAllister asked. "Those were Rebel pickets?"

"Yes, McAllister," the general replied. "Now Bobby Lee and the rest of the Reb army are short a few men. But we do need to move quickly now, before any alarm is raised."

Schoonover made a note to himself on how orderly and quietly this whole column of men (over one thousand pairs of feet) about faced and quickly returned to the original road. There, the entire column made a left turn and pushed on. It wasn't long before a crossroads was seen. Then, in the distance in front of them, there finally appeared countless numbers of camp-fires. Marching through the crossroads and on to the new road, the column filed past shadowy forms of peach trees, down a farm lane, and then into a broad meadow. They had at last found the Army of the Potomac.

In the gray early morning light, orders came down that, by regiment, the men were to find a place to rest. No sooner had they stopped, and the officers had them break out into companies, some collapsed from sheer exhaustion. Others had just enough energy to set up their shelter tents, crawl in, and sleep. The officers moved off to another part of the field to briefly meet before they, too, sought rest. The rest of the men were fast asleep as the barest hints of the new day, the last sunrise for so many began to show. The damp grass and other foliage welcomed them.

Cheston and Mount slipped off their gear and slumped to the ground. They laid their weapons right alongside them. For one of them this would be a last sunrise; the same for so many others who wore either blue or who wore gray.

Chapter Four
L I F E   O R   D E A T H

July 2, 1863

Mid-morning, the Trostle Farm

(Between Cemetery Ridge and the Emmitsburg Road)

M A J O R   G E N E R A L Daniel E. Sickles was not a happy man.
Angry. Frustrated. *Three* times this morning he'd shown three *different* officers the problem with the commanding General's orders for
his Corps! His requests for Meade to meet with him over where the
Third Corps was to be placed in line of battle apparently fell on deaf
ears.

He'd first shown Brigadier General Henry Hunt, Chief of Artillery of the Army of the Potomac, the major problems with his placement. Hunt agreed *in principle* with Sickles but did not have the
authority to over-ride the order. Then Sickles showed Brigadier General Gouverneur K. Warren the same position. Warren, the army's
Chief Engineer, also was in general agreement. Like Hunt, Warren
couldn't do anything either. Then along came Captain George
Meade, the commanding general's *own son,* who had the temerity
to ask why the Corps had not yet moved? Sickles sent the young officer back to Headquarters with the firm request for his father, the

General, to *personally* come out and see the horrible position the Corps would be in. *Good God,* Sickles fretted, *didn't Meade himself remember the disaster Chancellorsville turned into?*

While he waited for Meade to show up, Sickles grew more and more anxious by the moment. This even as several reports filtered in that Rebel infantry were in the Pitzer woods about a mile or two in front of him. And his own skirmishers sent out on reconnaissance had made contact. Skirmishing between both sides had occurred most of the morning; even now, it seemed to be increasing.

Sickles stewed, almost furious, even as he chomped on his ever-present cigar. Adding to his foul mood was his having to continually re-light the cigar. G_____, he thought to himself, *when is Meade, that high-and-mighty, google-eyed old snapping turtle, going to show? So I can show him how* bad *this position is?*

Major General David B. Birney, and Brigadier General Alexander A. Humphreys, his two division commanders, were not that far from him. Brigadier General Carr of Humphreys's Second Division, and Brigadier General Charles K. Graham of Birney's First Division, were also close by. All the other officers were looking at maps and using their field-glasses to match the terrain they were seeing with the maps.

Sighing in realization that Meade possibly might not even show up, Sickles turned to his two division commanders. "General Birney, and General Humphreys…a moment if you please?"

As Sickles cleared his throat and reached for a flask in his saddlebag for a healthy dose of *spiritus fermenti,* Colonel McAllister and Adjutant John Schoonover came riding up to the cluster of officers. They found them all situated on a small hillock in front of the stolid, brick-walled Trostle barn. McAllister and Schoonover climbed down off their horses and stood off a couple of feet away. Seeing them, Carr waved them over.

"Gentlemen," Sickles growled, "see that hill off to our left? It's a *very* prominent hill. If the _______ Rebs get hold of it, they can shell our present line." Pointing to where the Corps was lined up at the moment, he continued. "Remember Hazel Grove at Chancellorsville?" All the other officers in attendance nodded at the memory. "I need not tell all you gentlemen what a ______________ that was of Hooker ordering us to leave that hill. What you all do not know, is how *vehemently* I argued with General Hooker to rescind that order."

Sickles went on, taking care to point out both the road to the left of them and the peach orchard in the upper left distance. "Gentlemen, look at the terrain in front of you. We are going to move the entire Corps up to that higher ground you see before you. We will anchor our left flank on that road to your left that runs just in front of that peach orchard up there. Our right flank will be established and anchored along that road directly to your front, which also meets the road to your left at that peach orchard."

Now pointing to the map laid out before them, Sickles formalized his order. "I am ordering you to take the Corps and establish a line of infantry from the Corps and also fill in the gaps with artillery placed at good intervals."

Hearing that, McAllister and Schoonover looked at each other. Pulling Schoonover away from the group of officers, McAllister softly said, "Mr. Schoonover, please return to the regiment, present my compliments to the company commanders, and inform them we will be moving out shortly." Schoonover nodded, saluted, and quietly left.

McAllister turned back just in time to hear Sickles's next comments. "That hill of peach trees is the key to the position — *our position.* Our right will be a bit in the air so to speak, but we will anchor our left on the very hill the commanding General wants us to. In fact, we will be in front of it. We *must* deprive the Rebs of *that* high ground," Sickles said, jabbing his right arm toward the peach orchard.

"Gentlemen," Sickles asked, "any questions?" Seeing none raised, he continued, "Good...return to your commands, and prepare to advance forward to your new positions as soon as possible. Time is of the essence!"

With that, everyone else saluted their commander, mounted their horses, and moved out. McAllister mounted his horse and waited for Carr, his brigade commander, to join him.

Clearly worried, McAllister said, "General, sir? You *do* realize that if we go up there," pointing forward in the general direction of the road they could see running northwards toward Gettysburg, "we will be framed against the sky?"

Carr nodded in agreement. Continuing, McAllister said, "You do know, sir? It's going to be *one* dangerous place to be? With the fight that's surely coming?"

Carr looked at McAllister, his senior regimental commander and second in command of the brigade. "Colonel, it *is* the order. So, prepare your men to move."

"Yes, sir." McAllister saluted and then turned back toward his regiment. As he rode toward the Eleventh, he took the time to make a quick reconnaissance of the ground over which they'd maneuver, and most likely, fight.

July 2, 1863
Mid-afternoon, Gettysburg

"FALL IN!" McAllister roared the command at the top of his lungs, sweat streaming down his face. He took a handkerchief from inside his coat pocket and wiped it.

A groan went up from the men. Some of the men had to be encouraged with the blade of an officer's sword, or a nudge of a boot, or a vigorous shaking of shoulders. But the men formed into their companies, and then into the regiment. This was the *fourth* incidence of marching in the span of twenty-four hours, and the *second* time they'd moved this day. It was getting monotonous.

Both Cheston and Mount looked at each other. Up first, Cheston reached down and grabbed his friend's hand. "Come on, old man; up you go."

Mount moaned, "I am so tired; I can barely move!"

Standing nearby, Schoonover just smiled, and replied. "Come on, boys; this time…well, it's *for real*."

The colonel roared another order: *"Battalion, by company, fall in."* The men swiftly fell into line. There was no need for the officers to remind them to guide right. Once again, the knowledge gained from drill and now over a year of service together made this move possible by instinct. The company officers quickly gathered around McAllister and Schoonover to await their next orders.

To the assembled officers, McAllister said, "Have your companies strip for action, and then load weapons."

The orders were swiftly followed. Each man loaded his rifle, first pulling the cartridge from his cartridge box, tearing it open with the front teeth, pouring the gunpowder into the muzzle (the "business end"), and then removing the bullet itself from its wrapping and pressing it down with his right thumb until it was seated. The usual *thunks* and *kathunks* followed as the ramrod drove the bullet home. Finally, each man reached into his cap box for the percussion cap, placed on the nipple, and made sure the hammer was set at half-cock. To make sure the gun did not go off till it was needed. Then each man came to attention with his musket at the shoulder, as a sign he was loaded.

Ackerman called out, "Colonel, shall we have them fix bayonets, sir?"

"No," came McAllister's reply. "I suspect our initial contact will be at distance, and we shall have several volleys before we go to that!" *My God*, McAllister thought, *will it actually come to that???* To the color sergeant, he called out, "Sergeant, you will please uncover the colors!" And with that the colors were shaken out and fell limp in the dead summer air.

Brigadier General Joseph Carr approached on his horse. "Colonel, your regiment will be on the right of the brigade once we are in line of battle. Yours will be the further right flank of the division. Your regiment will be the rear-most battalion of the brigade, but the first to deploy into line!"

Seeing the other regiments already in column of battalions, the regiment fell into column in the rear of the brigade. At Carr's command of *"Attention, Battalions! Forward, March!"*, and with the command of *"March!"* repeated by the regimental commanders, and then the officers below them, the brigade began to slowly move. The bands of the brigade beat the cadence for the advance.

At first, McAllister thought about riding forward. He then reconsidered and fell into place with the color guard. The acrid burnt powder smoke smell from the cannons of both sides as well as the skirmishing that occurred almost since sunup drifted into his nostrils. As the brigade marched forward, it struck Ackerman that *this* was the way to go into battle. Flags flying—some snapping as a light breeze kicked up. The gleam of the rifle barrels as the sun shimmered off them. Then somewhere a band struck up the *Battle Cry of Freedom*. Slowly but surely everyone picked up the song.

The distance of over a mile now began to shrink. As they approached the rise before them, a collection of small farm buildings came into view. Then the command came to go from brigade column of battalions to regimental front of double lines. This was executed precisely, in almost parade ground fashion.

As the Eleventh neared the collection of farm buildings they'd seen, Carr came riding up. To McAllister, he said, "Colonel, your battalion will post *here* among this farm. You will support Seeley's battery to your right. More regiments are coming up and will be here shortly. Skirmishers from the Sixty-third Pennsylvania of Graham's brigade of the First Division as well as from our own division are to our entire front. So be careful; be aware of men returning and going out."

McAllister nodded, saluted, turned, and sought out Major Kearny. *God,* he thought, *Kearny is so young, but I have put him in command. I must trust him to do his job. Still, I wish we had Stephen Moore here with us. But this will have to do.* "Major!!!!!"

Kearny came up at a slow trot. "Major, have the battalion deploy into line of battle and take position among this farm up ahead. Once in position, you will have the battalion *lay down!*" No sooner had McAllister spoken, there was a loud *Booom* from across the fields to his left. Within seconds, a deafening *Kaaaboooom!* echoed as a shell exploded behind them. The men, who'd already deployed from column into line of battle, did not have to be told twice. They quickly hugged the ground, getting as low as they could in the dust and dirt.

Pounding hooves and the creak of wheels alerted him to the fact of Lieutenant Francis Seeley's Battery K, Fourth U.S. Artillery, arrival and unlimbering its six guns. Standing behind the regiment, McAllister watched as the artillerymen wrestled their guns into position. He thought to himself about how well drilled they were. It was only moments before the order to *Fire!* came. The entire battery loosed a salvo that caused the ground to jump and convulse under them.

Reload! came the command. Each gunner now sighted his piece; ordered the next round; the crews already sweating, swearing, as each gun was quickly sponged; the charge presented, rammed home. The order to prime, the primer inserted; the gunner's hand went up. *Ready!* came the next order. With the swift dropping of the hand came the command, *Fire!* Each piece seemed to explode — recoiling backwards, digging the trail into the ground flinging dirt, rock, powder residue backwards. Covering the front around them, bathing them in a fog of whitish gray smoke. Wiping out for a moment the scene before them.

A *Booom* was followed by the *whirrrrrrr* sound a shell makes in flight. All eyes caught the shell in midair as it headed toward their position. As it reached the highest part of its flight, it seemed to hesitate. It then plunged to the ground with a great roaring sound, and *Kaaaabooooom!* The shell exploded directly to their front, showering McAllister and the color guard with dirt and unblown bits of powder. "Steady, boys," Ackerman was heard to say. "Steady! There is no safer place than where you are! Steady!!!!"

McAllister motioned to Major Kearny as a reminder for every one of the officers to get down. And even he fell to one knee. He pulled his field binoculars from his side and swung them to his eyes. *By the Almighty, I must remember to load my own pistol!* he thought out loud. Waving Sgt. Major Tilton over and handing the man his pistol and cartridge box, McAllister said, "Would you be so kind to please do me the honor of loading this pistol for me??" As requested, the sergeant major loaded the proffered weapon, and handed it back to his commander. Giving off a quick salute, he returned to his proper position.

The artillery fire ratcheted up in intensity; there was more frequent firing from the Rebel guns across the way. Seeley's Battery on the left of the house and then Turnbull's Battery on the other side of the house joined in. To the south, in among what looked to be peach trees, artillery guns there were put to the task, erupting every moment or so in gray smoke tinted by bright orange, red, or yellow flashes as each shell went hurtling toward its target.

Another sound greeted McAllister's ears. The sound of glass breaking as men from two of the nearby regiments took up position in the farmhouse. He heard even the thudding and creaking noises as the mud and straw insulation between the logs of the home were chipped out, creating slits. The home was being turned into a temporary fortress.

The frequency of the shelling grew more pronounced with each passing moment. The artillery exchange became one continuous roar. The very air was filled with shells, the screams of wounded animals, the curses of the gun crews, the moans of the wounded men—all while leaf petals from the apple orchard they were in rained down on them.

All of this, this great dynamic mixture, created a tableau that, as time wore on, kept changing. An explosion of a shell there; the report of a gun over there; the smell of sweat, blood, fear; the desperate need of men trying to get lower, making themselves part of the earth they believed they had come out of, digging fingers, feet, *anything* to get lower. All of this creating a great, ever-changing mosaic of sound and color.

The regiment by now had changed places at least three times. Finding itself at a forty-five-degree angle (an oblique angle in military terms), up against the barn, almost touching. The barn's red walls served as all but a backdrop to the drama before them. McAllister noted his position. One of Carr's staff had just left with further orders. They were to hold, and stay, and fight this out. *We are in such a dangerous place,* he thought to himself. *How do we hold?* The One-hundred-and-twentieth New York had fallen in on their left flank; the small Fifth New Jersey was near the house; several men from the Twelfth New Hampshire had already taken up residence in the house itself.

At that very moment, an aide from Sewell's staff came running, out of breath, amid the din. "Begging the Colonel's pardon," he said, between gasps for air. "Begging…"

"Easy, soldier; easy, what is it?" McAllister calmly asked.

"Sir, Colonel Sewell is down, and badly wounded, along with Lieutenant Seeley and several of our men, all down. Andddd…"

"Easy, my good man, easy! Soldier, out with it!"

"Sir, the skirmishers from our regiment have come running back, yelling there are Rebs coming. *Thick as fleas, sir!* We could see them clearly as they stepped out of the woods across the way. Well sir, we are not sure; begging your pardon, sir; *what do we do???* Seeley's battery is pulling out from its position in the road…and…"

This poor boy, this man needs to rest, but I need to know! What should we do? McAllister thought, trying to make sense of the now-changed situation. Quickly pulling out his field glasses and scanning the fields of the farm across the road and the advancing Rebels, McAllister made a decision.

"Son, tell your commanding officer to draw close to the flank of the Twelfth New Hampshire, and pull the Twenty-sixth Pennsylvania in closer in as well!"

"But Colonel," the young officer said, "our right flank, sir; it's in the air! And the Rebs, sir!" In a panicked outburst, he continued, "The Rebs, *they are coming from across the road!*" A line or two of the enemy abruptly charged ahead, seeking to capture Seeley's retiring guns. Suddenly another voice called down from an upstairs window of the farmhouse, "Here they come, sir!" In an alarmist tone, the soldier yelled again, *"Here they come!"* With that, the troops to the right exploded with a volley of musketry against the advancing Rebels.

The musketry sounded like a thunderclap. The guns in the house began to spit out shots. It was fast becoming total chaos.

McAllister saw the unmistakable Confederate battle flags defiantly waving in the distance before him. "Major Kearny," McAllister yelled over the chaotic noise. *"Major Kearny!!!"* Again, he roared above this incredible, deafening, ringing collection of sound. Suddenly it seemed he was in a small room somewhere; the sounds bounced off the walls of both the barn and the house, trying to overwhelm his senses. *I need to keep my head clear, steady,* he thought. *Steady…*

Kearny showed up at a run. "Yes, Colonel? What are your orders, sir?"

"*Major!* "McAllister bellowed again, making sure he could be heard. "We need to take our two right companies and refuse them, putting them parallel to the road! We have another threat coming *right at us*! Do you understand me???"

"*Yes, sir!*" was Kearny's reply. With that, he spun on his heels to get those two right companies placed in position as ordered.

In the midst of all of this, the blinding smoke, the sounds of complete battle, he found himself thinking: *If it wasn't for the fact that men, souls being maimed, and killed, ushered into eternity, I find this all perfectly magnificent!* He quickly shook his head to clear it of the very thought, to get his mind on it all.

He looked south, and the scene before him less than 300 yards away was mass confusion. Caissons exploding; horses rearing in their death throes, men trying to get the animals under control so they could pull the guns off and out of danger; gun crews hooking up the prolong ropes to their guns and as the guns went off, they manually pulled the guns back. Loading them again to repeat this, to get their guns out of harm's way. There was a yelp and a cheer, a huzzah and then cheers, as a regiment under its colors charged the d______e Rebels in their front. Men spinning, spitting blood before falling; horses toppling in their own death throes; adding to this all, screams of the Rebel yell; and yes, they *were* turning, they *were* coming his way. The One-hundred-and-twentieth New York, closer to the advancing enemy, triggered a volley. It received one in return, causing men to tumble in different contorted heaps. There were Rebel officers on horseback; one who had long flowing gray hair was driving his men forward. But he headed further east, or at least he seemed to be. Red and blue uniforms ran toward the Eleventh's position, turning to fire, only to fall to the ground like rag dolls.

The Rebels to the south were now about 250 yards away. The time had come for his regiment to join the fight. *"Rise up, Jerseymen!"* McAllister shouted above the din. *"Ready!"* came his next order. *"Fire by battalion! Commence firing!"* At the colonel's command, the company commanders shouted, *"Company! Ready! Aim!"* The rattle of equipment and the rustle of clothing was heard as each soldier brought his weapon to bear. *"Steady, boys, and aim low!!"* As the companies readied to let loose their first volley, McAllister shouted, *"Now,* men; now's the time! Give them *everything* you've got! *Fire!!!"*

The first volley delivered; McAllister lifted his sword. *"By rank! Rear rank first!"* The company officers echoed his orders. *"Rear rank! Ready! Aim!"* Again, he shouted above the vast deep confusing noise. *"Fire!!!"* was his next command; the weapons seemed to pour out a solid wall of flame. It sounded like a heavy rain falling on a tin roof. All at once. A deluge of flame, smoke, and noise. All rolled into one.

Then it was the front rank's turn. *"Rear rank, load! Front rank, kneel! Ready, aim, fire!!"* McAllister bellowed; another roar, another thunderclap, as the rifles exploded in a volley of musketry. Adding that noise to the increasingly deafening kaleidoscope of this bedlam of mortal combat.

"Load, men, load! "McAllister bellowed again. The officers repeated his order, almost as loud as his, taking courage from his stern commands.

Like a lion, he roared again. *"Attention, Battalion! By company, by files right, fire!"* Another volley of musketry rang out, but this time like a large dog barking, each soldier's weapon fired in succession. The men did not have to be told what to do next. It was automatic. Load musket, tear off the top of the cartridge, pour the powder down the barrel, insert the bullet itself, ram it home, bring the musket up so the cap could be placed on the nipple cone, then the hammer to full cock... and fire. As the men reloaded, the colonel took a step back, so he could see what was going on in front of both parts of his regiment. To let the smoke clear.

Kaaablaammmm!!! Knocked off his feet, McAllister was thrown to the ground like a rag doll. In the same moment, the inside of his left thigh just above the knee felt as if someone plunged a white-hot knife into his leg, and turned it on its hilt. Simultaneously, his right foot throbbed as if hit with a sledgehammer. It pulsed with almost overwhelming pain. He thought immediately of his beloved wife and daughters. He prayed, *"Lord Jesus, please save me! Please! Oh my..."* He bit his tongue as the waves of pain rolled over him.

"Colonel!" He heard someone cry out. And then there were men around him. "Colonel, are you all right?"

"No!" he squeaked. "No! Check my left leg and right foot. I have been hit and hurt mortally I fear!"

Another friendly face appeared. "Colonel, sir, you have been hit and it looks bad." It was Mount. The lieutenant grabbed his colonel's hand. "Sir, we *must* get you off this field!"

"Get a tourniquet around my leg," McAllister said, gasping in pain. "I don't want to bleed to death!"

"Sir," Mount said, "we must get you to the rear!" With that, three others appeared. Together with Mount, each one grabbed the colonel under his shoulders and his legs to move him rearward. At that, McAllister passed out.

Schoonover saw the commotion. *Somebody is down? Who?* He felt a hand on his shoulder; he turned to see Major Kearny. Kearny had a funny grin on his face, and said, "We are going to have one hell of a fight, are we not?" Just then, *Thwaaack!* As a round slammed into his knee, Kearny screamed in pain. As Kearny spun away from the impact, Schoonover looked to his right and saw a gravely wounded McAllister being carried toward the rear. *The Colonel's down; the Major's down,* John thought. *That means Ackerman is now in command.*

As he headed toward the regiment's senior Captain to pass on the news of the command change, Schoonover heard another sound. It was more of a crunch, and he saw Ackerman grab his sleeve. The other officer's eyes rolled back in his head. He slowly slumped downward, dead before he hit the ground; his premonition back in Gum Springs fulfilled.

Oh, my God, this is crazy! Schoonover thought to himself. *All right, I must keep myself together!* Schoonover's mind raced. *THREE senior officers down…who is next?*

At that moment, with the men firing as they were ready, they began to fall. Screams, groans, cheers, huzzahs, curse-filled shouts as men loaded and fired independently. The men gave out as good as they received. And, amidst all the lead coming in at them, that damnable Rebel yell filled the air.

Jake Mount and Joey Cheston fought together. Suddenly Mount felt a tug on his arm. Cheston looked at him, a growing red spot appearing on the upper portion of his shirt. "Jake, I am afraid I am a goner…Please remember me to my beloved…*Pleaseee!*" he groaned in his agony. Mount eased his friend to the ground.

"Jake," he gasped, struggling for breath. "Please find the photo, inside my coat! Please!" Jake did as his friend asked.

"Thank you," Cheston said. He grabbed the photo and kissed that beloved face. Then his eyes rolled back in his head, and he was gone.

"Nooooo!!!!" Jake yelled, *"No!!!!!!!!!!!"* With that he picked up Joe's musket and pulled the trigger right into the face of an onrushing Rebel. The man's face just melted away. *Gotcha, you d____d grayback!* He picked up his own gun, aimed, and pulled the trigger again. The gun roared and leapt in his hands. He was now a mad man, bent on revenging his best friend's death. Loading and firing; loading and firing. When his gun fouled, he picked up Cheston's and kept right on fighting. His face and lips turned blacker with every cartridge torn open, every round loaded. He thrust his ramrod into the ground in as much of an act of outright defiance to the hated Rebels as noting where he could stand and fight. It was no longer a

fight to preserve the Union or to free the slaves. It was *personal* to him now.

Schoonover noticed all of this. But he also noted, to himself, *I don't have time to be remorseful, that will come later! Come on, John!* he said to himself. *THINK! What would the Colonel do?*

Looking left, he noticed both Captains Lloyd and Martin go down, get up, and be helped to the rear. Another artillery round exploded behind the line. *I must do something about that!*

In two steps he was at the side of the corporal who held the national colors. "Corporal Johnson!" he yelled above the increasing crescendo of noise. "I need you to go twenty yards in front of the line and plant the colors! I am going to pull the regiment back by twenty yards. I know it's an odd order, but we *must* get the artillery off us!"

Johnson just nodded, gulped, hugged the colors to his body, and advanced those twenty yards over the bodies of the color guard who had already been killed.

As Schoonover had the regiment fall back twenty yards, the artillery fire shifted. More casualties, more men going down. *So quickly…* he thought. *If we stay here much longer, we will not have a regiment left!*

"Battalion!" he shouted at the top of his lungs, yelling so loud it startled him. Every man looked at him. *"Dress your ranks! Right shoulder shift, Arms! About, Face! By the double quick, March! Close up, men; close up!"*

He turned to see if all the other men had heard him. At that moment, he felt he had been punched in the chest, knocking him down to his knees. He stayed there for a moment, coughing, trying to catch his breath. He shook his head to clear it, started to get up — only to feel like someone punched him in the shoulder, bashing him down again. This time he stood up, grabbed his arm, flexed it, and picked up his sword. Over to his left, he saw an officer ride up to a cluster of his men, point at a Rebel officer on horseback, gesturing with much emphasis. All seven of the men leveled their weapons at the officer and fired, knocking him from the saddle.

He felt a helping hand grip him in the armpit, helping him to steady himself. He turned to see the face of Captain Samuel Sleeper.

"Well, Mr. Schoonover," Sleeper shouted, "it looks like you command the regiment. I am in no shape to do so. What is your order?"

Schoonover took a moment to take in the carnage around him.

"Captain, sir, we need to retire the regiment from the field. Where are the colors?" *Damn,* he thought to himself, *I forgot him!*

"Captain, stay here for the moment!" Above the din of mortal combat, he shouted, "Eleventh New Jersey!! Rally to the Captain and the colors! Rally, men!!! *Rally!!*" As he raced off back toward the farm, at that moment he could see the Rebel battle flags coming triumphantly, defiantly across the road.

He ran up to the back of the barn to peer around a corner. And felt a tug at his sleeve. "Here I am, Lieutenant! I took cover so our colors wouldn't be lost!" said Johnson.

Schoonover managed a weak smile. "Thank God, you are okay! Please follow me!" At the run, they both took off toward where Schoonover thought he'd left Captain Sleeper. Out of what seemed to be a cloud of smoke, he found the regiment. Or, what was left of it.

"Rally to the Colors!" he shouted, swinging his sword in a circle in the air. "Rally to me!!!"

With that, the tattered remains of this faithful few of the regiment collected on the colors. Schoonover led them back about ten yards. Had them turn...and fire. He repeated it. Turn and fire. Another ten yards. Turn and fire. Slowly but surely, they retreated toward the very thicket they had marched so grandly through. *Was it just moments ago?* Schoonover thought to himself.

Finally, they came to the thicket. Schoonover yelled for them to find cover among the big rocks and any other cover that was there. Including a thickly covered fence line of rails and bushes. There, the regiment—or its survivors—gathered its breath, took a sip from a dirty stream just to moisten and clean out their parched, dirty mouths or to do a hurried swab out of their musket barrels. The Rebels were still pushing them, but even they halted to recover and reform.

John looked to the other side of this thicket. Off in the distance, he saw another unit marching forward to help stem the Confederate tide. To his left, he also noticed an artillery battery firing almost as fast as they loaded their guns. They were in a semi-circle in the front yard of another farm. To the rear was another battery setting up on a ridgeline. When the second battery was ready, both batteries then fired a collective salvo. Farther back—it almost seemed *so far,* for it was going to be over open ground, was a line of artillery setting up. And there were what looked to be infantry flags among them. There, *there* was safety. *There* was the place to go…

"Men!!! Attention, men…As soon as you can, head to the guns behind us. Do not stop to fire, do that when you make the artillery line!!! When I say *Retreat,* I want everyone on your feet and to run like the Devil himself is after you!!"

"On your feet, men!" He yelled at the top of his lungs. "*Retreat!!*" With that, everyone who could move, ran for dear life. Those who couldn't had help from others. The startled Rebels paused. It was like flushing a covey of quail back home.

What was left of the Eleventh, and even some of the other regiments who had fought so valiantly, joined in this retreat. They covered the open ground quickly; the battery on the rise giving them cover. And they fell among the guns, gasping for air. Safe for now. Off to their right, they all noticed a regiment rush forward with a huzzah. Unsure of what this new movement meant; the advancing Rebels stopped cold. They recovered in time to deliver a withering volley into the Union troops. And then crept closer, closer. Until the Union batteries let loose with a devastating blast of canister and double canister. All of this caused the Rebel advance to slow. Then they, too, had enough, and retreated in some confusion to where they'd advanced from.

Schoonover rested on the wheel of one of the caissons of an artillery piece. Gasping. Suddenly there was a commotion. A lieutenant from one of the other regiments stepped forward. John recognized him as Lieutenant Fennell from the Twelfth New Hampshire. Fennell stood in front of the tattered, shattered group of what was left of three Union brigades. He drew his sword, and yelled, *"Who will follow me??? Come on, boys! Let us get the ground back! Fix, bayonets! Charge, bayonets!!!"*

There was a collective grunt. *"Charge!"* was Fennell's roar. These tired, battered men surged forward, colors from so many regiments, all mingled together. With a yip and a *Huzzah,* they lowered their muskets, and charged. Into history.

Schoonover was spent. He stood there and watched them go. He could not take another step. He was done. He sank to the ground, exhausted, tears streaming down his face. For him, the fight was over.

July 2,1863
Evening, Cemetery Ridge

McAllister lay on his cot, alternately losing and regaining consciousness. He fought the overwhelming pain, trying desperately to stay alert to what occurred around him. The air was filled with the smell of blood, mingled with the odor of sweat, and the musty scent of the tent. Next to him was the prostrate form of Phil Kearny. A groan occasionally escaped the young officer's lips as he, too, tried to cope with his own pain and suffering.

A slight breeze came gently in through the open tent flap, and with it came a form whose face began to come into focus. The visitor checked first to see how McAllister's bandages were holding, and then a glance at his swollen foot. It appeared the bleeding had stopped there as well.

"Colonel, sir," Surgeon Welling said. "Colonel, you need to have something to drink. And you need something for pain. Would you please take some whiskey, as I have no other means by which to deal with it for you?"

McAllister shook his head. "No, sir; I do not partake. Thank you for offering!"

"Well, Colonel, there are two more wounded in front of you, and I will be back to take Major Kearny shortly. I will check on you again then!"

"Thank you, Edward! Thank you!" McAllister said weakly.

McAllister kept fading in and out of consciousness, getting weaker as the evening wore on. So much so, he didn't even notice when the two men came to pick up Kearny, until that familiar face of the surgeon appeared over him.

"Colonel…Colonel…Sir…Please, sir, it will not be long, and you need refreshment! Please take some whiskey, or at least water!"

McAllister, his lips and his throat rasping from thirst, shook his head to the first, but muttered, "Water, a bit of water, yes…but see to the Major first, please!"

"Colonel, the Major is on his way to the table. I will send for water."

Welling was gone but a moment as it seemed, when McAllister felt his head being lifted and water being ever so gently poured over his dried, cracked lips. Even though it was warm, it was refreshing. He sank back onto his bed after a few moments, exhausted from even the small task of drinking water.

Time seemed to go ever so slowly, the faces of Ellen and the two girls swirling before him. He found himself calling out their names, and then the faces of so many others. Moore, Schoonover, Ackerman, the other officers — even the faces of some of those who had been killed at Chancellorsville, swam before his eyes. His leg throbbed now; his foot pulsed with a stabbing pain. And then — that face again, and its familiar voice. The voice of Surgeon Edward Welling.

"Colonel, Colonel; you are next and I have no means to make you comfortable. Would you please, *pleaseee*, take some whiskey!"

Even though he was now so weak, McAllister murmured, "Surgeon, I cannot, as it's against my convic…." He didn't finish the sentence.

"Colonel, sir, will you take some milk?"

McAllister barely opened his eyes and shook his head yes.

"Good, then! Orderlies! Take him to the table. The Colonel is next up, and I will get the milk for him."

Welling was exhausted himself, but knew he *had* to keep on, to keep going. He admired and cared for the colonel so deeply that he *had* to find a way. He quickly walked to where he had laid his own medical pack down, pulled out a container of his personal stock, and filled a tin cup half full of whiskey. He then headed to the commissary wagon.

"Sergeant, I need some milk…" Crisp looked at him, and a slight smile crept across his face. He knew who this was for. "For the Colonel?" At a nod from Welling, he said, "I have some for him. Special milk, fresh from a local Pennsylvania cow this very morning!" And with a wink, filled the cup the rest of the way.

Careful to not spill a drop of the precious liquid, Welling briskly walked back the short distance to the regimental field hospital. Near a small white house not far from the Taneytown road. *Well, it was where they were treating the wounded,* he noted. *Some hospital it was! Under a damn tree! Open air!*

He found the colonel on the table, pant leg ripped open to the groin, the foot propped up, waiting his skilled hands. But first the "milk."

"Colonel, Colonel; here is the milk you said you drink, but you must down it all!"

The orderlies, and some others who were standing nearby, got McAllister into somewhat of a sitting position. "Down the hatch you go, sir!" McAllister downed the cup in gulps, and as he finished, a smile creased his face. To Welling, he said, "Oh my, what wonderfully tasting milk!" And he was out like a light.

For the second time in the last few days, Crisp — who this time had followed Welling back — said to the unconscious form of his colonel: "Sleep well, me Colonel darlin', sleep well!" And Welling went to work.

Welling wiped his hands on his bloody apron and grabbed hold of the probe he needed to examine the leg. *The foot can wait,* Welling muttered. *But this leg, we better deal with this,* he found himself saying. Carefully he lifted the leg and looked for the wound. Just inside the thigh. *Good, easy to reach; now let's see what we have,* he said out loud, like it really helped him to focus on the task at hand.

"Orderly, hold the leg tight please! And you, Mr. Mount, please have bandages ready just in case. I don't know if the bullet is resting on an artery or a blood vessel. An artery, hell, he will not survive more than five minutes if it is!" With that he took off the bandage and examined the wound.

"Well, I will be damned," he said, in pleasant surprise. For right at the surface of the wound was the bullet—no, make that a round ball. It looked to be too large to come from a musket; it had to be canister or even from an exploding shell. Ever so carefully he inserted the probe, got it under the projectile, and slowwwwly popped the round out! He quickly stuffed a bandage into the open wound for a moment. *Good, no gushing geyser of blood, so no artery or even a vein,* he thought.

"Colonel, even though you can't hear me," Welling said, "you were saved by Divine Providence! You are one fortunate man, sir!" He plopped the round into a pan close by. *On to the foot,* he said to himself. The orderly began to bandage up the leg.

McAllister's boots had been either removed or cut off. One boot looked like someone had taken a knife to it and cut the sole of it right off, peeling it back to the heel. Welling looked it over for a quick moment and determined it did not give him any clues as to the nature of the wound itself. He picked the foot up and looked at the sole. Again, the colonel had been a fortunate man. All the miles they had marched and all the time he had insisted he walk with the men had saved him. Although the foot was badly bruised on the bottom, it had already turned a deep purple and red with even a tint of yellow around the edge. The calloused foot looked more like a small, overripe melon. Welling again found himself shaking his head. *The Colonel had to have someone watching over him,* Welling thought. *Or his clean living had saved him.* Welling found he was smiling to himself. *This is one man that was going to keep all his limbs. And, providing no infection set in, he* would *return to command.* That was the best news all day. He would share that with McAllister when the Colonel woke up.

"Orderly! Take the Colonel back to his tent. Make sure you keep an eye on him. I do think it is going to be all right…*thank God!*"

McAllister awoke to see Schoonover leaning over him.

"Colonel, Colonel! It's me, Lieutenant Schoonover!"

McAllister blinked his eyes several times, licked his lips. *Oh, what a headache!* He thought. "Water! Please, water," he said with a raspy voice. Schoonover seemed to pull a canteen from somewhere, and lifted McAllister's head so he could drink.

"Here you are, sir!"

Schoonover then yelled, "Orderly!" The orderly appeared as out of nowhere. "Please get the Surgeon; tell him the Colonel is awake."

Schoonover turned back to McAllister. "Sir, you came through surgery well. You kept your leg, and your foot—though swollen— will heal over time. You have always, sir, insisted that the Lord God will look out for us. You will be all right, sir."

Welling appeared just then. "Well, Colonel, God has certainly saved your life! You will be a while recovering, but barring any in-fection, you should be well."

"Thank you, Dr. Welling," McAllister said. Welling turned and left.

"Lieutenant!"

"Yes, sir!" Schoonover said.

McAllister asked, "How is the regiment? Is it still together? How bad was our loss?"

Schoonover let out a long, sorrowful sigh. "We suffered heavily, sir. The count is still being totaled as the regiment ended up a bit scattered. The number of those still standing is uncertain. We esti-mate it at only one-hundred left standing, and even those all seem to have a wound of some kind."

"Officers…How many did we lose?" McAllister said in that dry voice, barely above a whisper.

"Well, sir," Schoonover answered. "Captain Sleeper is the only com-pany commander still standing if one calls it that. And even *he* is hurt."

McAllister closed his eyes, a tear formed on his cheek. "That means we have lost Kearny, Lloyd, Martin, Ackerman, all the com-pany commanders?"

"Yes, sir; I fear so, sir. Now, Colonel, you *must* rest."

McAllister's lower lip quivered. "Yes, I must rest...."

Schoonover bent over his Colonel, and lightly touched his lips to his forehead. "Yes, Colonel, darling," just like he had heard the old Commissary Sergeant say so many times, "you rest easy. Rest easy, sir!"

From a shadowy corner of the tent stepped Lt. Mount. "Colonel, sir; Colonel!"

"Who is this?" McAllister asked.

"It's me, Colonel, sir; Lieutenant Mount..."

"Oh, good. Lieutenant, you need to return to the regiment!"

"With all due respect, Colonel," Mount said. "I am needed *here*. And will be here if you need anything."

"All right then!"

"You are welcome, sir!" Mount said, and retreated into the corner where he came from. McAllister closed his eyes, trying to sleep.

Schoonover walked out of the tent and approached Surgeon Welling.

"Doc," he asked, "where can I find Kearny?"

Welling responded, "Over next to the fence line, under a tree. He is resting but is tormented by pain. I have nothing to help him other than whiskey, so he is in and out of consciousness. Be patient with him." Schoonover nodded, and in a few short steps found him.

"Kearny," he gently shook his shoulder as he leaned over him. "Kearny..." Kearny slowly turned toward Schoonover; his eyes almost glazed over from pain. "Schoonover? Is that you?"

John replied. "Yes, Major; it is me. I wanted to look in on you." Despite the awful pain, Kearny found the will to reply.

"Well, the Rebs got me good. Took my leg. Right at the knee." He coughed, grimaced at the same time. "Doc Welling tells me I may recover, but I will do so in a hospital near home in New York. Will be headed there shortly...John...*John!*"

"Yes, I am here," Schoonover said. "What can I get you? What do you need?"

"Please, John," Kearny replied, "see to it that my mother gets my letters. They are in my knapsack, over there. Please do that for me, will you?"

"Yes, Major. I will. You take care of yourself. And rest easy as well."

Kearny could not see the tears in Schoonover's eyes as he turned away. All of this was ripping Schoonover apart inside. More than he ever realized.

July 2, 1863
Moments later, Cemetery Ridge,
Near the center of the Army's position.

Schoonover slowly dismounted from his horse. There was not a part of him that didn't hurt. He was beyond exhausted. Sgt. Crisp took hold of the reins and asked in low tones: "How is the Colonel? Kearny?"

Schoonover muttered, "Both are in bad shape. Doc Welling says McAllister will live, but Kearny…Well, it's going to be an exceedingly *long* recovery. He lost a leg below the knee."

The sergeant muttered something about Divine Providence in reply.

Schoonover walked slowly over to where a cluster of camp-fires were burning. Spotting what looked to be a company guidon that he could not quite make out, he approached. The Eleventh's state colors slowly flapped in the slight breeze, marking where what was left of the leadership of the regiment could be found.

Captain Sleeper slowly, painfully stood up. Obviously, he was hurting as well. He held out his hand as if to welcome Schoonover back. John just held up his right hand as if to say he was all right but, well, had had enough.

"Lieutenant," Sleeper said, "a member of Birney's staff just left. He wanted to know who was in command of the regiment. I told him I was not able to continue as I am not in good shape. I told him *you* were the man for the job! And you would be up to the task."

Schoonover sighed. "All right, Captain. Yes. I guess I shall have to. Right?"

"Well, Lieutenant," Sleeper answered, "you are the highest-ranking officer next to me. You are the one."

At that moment, the sound of horses' hooves resounded over the packed earth. Several riders were approaching. *Who could this be?* Schoonover thought. Still standing, he turned to face in the direction of the newcomers.

It was Major General Birney himself, now in command of the Third Corps. Or what was left of it. And some of his staff. He halted in front of the camp-fire which lit up all their faces. Birney's once clean uniform was dusty dirty, filthy for that matter; he had been in the saddle for most of this horrible day. Especially after Sickles being severely wounded earlier in the fight, and getting slightly wounded himself.

"Are you Schoonover?" Birney asked.

"Yes, sir; I am," with a salute that Birney returned.

"Well, Lieutenant," Birney said, looking down at him from his horse. "Sir, you are now in *temporary* command of this regiment."

A cold chill ran up his back, as he remembered his thoughts on that long-ago day in August of 1862. The thing he feared the most had happened; he now had the responsibility of what was left of the Eleventh.

"Yes, sir!" Schoonover saluted, after getting over the shock of the "instant" promotion. "Yes, sir; I will do my best, sir!"

Birney returned the salute. "Good luck, *Lieutenant;* you will need it." Continuing, he said: "Schoonover, I will send orders as to what I want you to do with your regiment in the morning. For now, find out what you have left, and appoint the appropriate men to take over the companies. Send the list to me and I will approve the promotions."

Birney flipped another salute at Schoonover and at all present. He then turned and faded back into the night from which he came.

John returned to the camp-fire. He ran his hand through his matted hair, and then pulled a handkerchief from his vest pocket.

He found the handkerchief full of holes from the shotgun blast that knocked him down earlier. He chuckled. *Now there is a sight for you!*

He then went to pull his coat off. As he did so, those around the camp-fire gasped, and shook their heads. John stared at them all with this befuddled look on his face. He wasn't sure if they were reacting to the news of his instant promotion.

"What's the matter?"

Sleeper responded, "Sir, look at the hem of your coat!"

John held it up to the flickering light of the camp-fire. The hem was shot away, totally in tatters. The bottom edges of the coat were so damaged from the rounds that passed through it, that no seamstress (or the best one in the army) could even attempt to repair it.

Near the Klingel Farm...
About the same time

The angry sun set over the battlefield, almost furious at the devastation it beheld. Its last, fading rays basked the ghastly scene in a reddish glow. Jake Mount had gone back toward the Klingel farm, looking for his friend Joseph Cheston. He started up by the house, almost to the road, slowly turning over bodies, pushing gray- and butternut-clad men off blue-clad bodies. He looked into the faces of men who were now nothing but pale ghosts of their former selves. Their forms already were turning black as the summer heat began the work of returning them to the earth. As he looked for his friend, tears dripped off his face. "Joe," he sobbed, "where are you? Come on, Joe!"

At almost that instant, a voice — seemingly out of nowhere in the darkening twilight — startled him. At first, he thought one of the bodies around him made a sound. The voice called out in a very deep Southern drawl, "What'r ye doin' thar, Billy Yank?"

"Huh? Wha...?" was Jake's startled reply, thinking perhaps he heard a ghost. Straightening his aching body, he turned to see three scruffy looking figures clad in dirty gray and butternut standing not far away. Holding their rifles ready if needed, but half pointing in Jake's direction and half at the ground.

"I'm…I'm looking," he stammered out, "for my best friend, who went down during the fighting earlier here. Probably 'gainst some of you fellers."

Once again in a deep Southern drawl, one of the rebels noted, "Waal, we-uns is from 'bama on picket duty hyar."

Another one of the Rebels then spoke up. "We-uns saw ye movin' about, turnin' bodies ovuh. Waal, we-uns'r simply curious."

Jake turned to face them full on. There was enough left of twilight for the three Rebels to see his face. Jake's face wore the look of a broken-hearted, deeply grieving, young man. His tears had formed rivulets of moisture down his begrimed, powder- and battle-stained face.

In a shock of recognition of *why* Jake was there, one of the Rebels who'd not spoken before, said, "*Ohhhhh.* Okay, Billy, we-uns will let ye be."

It dawned on Jake he and the three Rebels were all about the same age. Way too young to be trying to kill each other. The Rebel continued, in a tone that was more of compassion than hostility, "We-uns won't bother ye none, iffn ye don't bother us-uns!"

"Thank ya kindly, Johnny Reb," Jake said. "I *really* need to find my friend."

With that, one of the other Rebels gave Jake a sort of friendly salute, saying: "Well, we-uns hope yuh find 'im." And, as quickly as they'd appeared, they faded back into the dusky twilight they'd come out of. *Almost like ghosts.*

Jake resumed his frantic search. He finally, finally rolled another soldier over. And there lay his dear friend, his mess and tent mate. Jake slid to the ground, picking up his friend's remains in a bear hug, crying and wailing with what seemed to be his whole being.

"Oh, Joe! Joe! Why, *why??*" he sobbed. "Please, oh please, don't go! What will I tell Beverly? *What will I say to her?*" The sobs racked his body. His whole being just shook with his sobbing. "Oh no, not you Joe, oh please...Not you...Oh, God! Almighty God, why him? *Whyyyy?"*

Jake's wailing rang across the field as darkness settled in. The crickets and the moans of the wounded and dying blended in, joining in this macabre scene. All night long this went on. Even as the details came, with their lanterns. They mingled in with the fireflies and showed a scene none would soon forget. The remains of thousands of men, lying where they fell. In some cases, in perfect rows where they dropped. The more one looked, the more the scene went on and on and on.

A detail of Union soldiers looking for wounded eventually found Jake, still cradling the body of his dead friend. Jake had fallen asleep from exhaustion. One of the soldiers shook him, wakening him with a start. For a long moment, he didn't know where he was. Then, reality returned; he remembered. Looking up at one of the soldiers in the detail, he said, "This is my best friend Joseph Cheston, Company C, Eleventh Regiment, New Jersey Volunteers. Would you see that he gets a proper burial?"

The soldier who'd awakened Jake nodded, replying, "We'll bury him here. Would you like to help?"

"No," Jake said. "I can't; I can't. I can't bear it. But, thank you kindly for your compassion."

Slowly getting to his feet, Jake Mount trundled back to the remnant of his regiment. He thanked God that, somehow, he was still alive after this day and vowed to never forget his dear friend as long as he lived. *Never...*

Chapter Five
REMEMBRANCE
AND DEDICATION

June 28, 1888

Gettysburg...the last train stop

S C R E E E E C C C H H H ... The train chugged and groaned to a halt. The conductor came into their car. "Gettysburg, this stop! Gettysburg! End of the line!"

Schoonover and Elizabeth collected their belongings; the two boys took their cues from their parents. As the entire party slowly exited the car and the train, the slanting rays of the early evening sun hinted at a warmer day on the morrow.

They were met on the train platform by what seemed to be a blur of people. The governors of New Jersey and of Pennsylvania introduced themselves, as did the commissioners of the New Jersey State Gettysburg Battlefield Commission. The dedication of the New Jersey monuments was the reason the entire Schoonover family made the long journey. They climbed into the carriage that would be their transportation to their hotel where they were honored guests. John spent part of that night making sure his remarks would be persuasive and flowed well.

Then, during the early morning hours of June 29, he departed the hotel and took the horse provided for him to ride along the Emmitsburg Road. As he headed down that road to make the turn onto Wheatfield Road at the now-famous Peach Orchard, he passed the scenes of the fighting on July second almost twenty-five years before. He quickly noticed the monument to his former regiment, suitably covered, awaiting its solemn dedication on the next day.

Once John reached the now-famous Wheatfield, he took over command of the veteran camp of the 1,600 officers and men who were there to help dedicate the monuments to the heroic services of New Jersey troops on that field. He made sure all those in attendance were as comfortable as they could be. He found, however, the old veterans were happy to be back together on such an auspicious occasion. A special provisional regiment composed of men and officers from the New Jersey National Guard was also camped nearby. That regiment was there acting as escorts for the governors of New Jersey and Pennsylvania, invited dignitaries, and the veterans in attendance.

The next day, June 30, was the one for which John had waited for five long years. In the early afternoon, the entire family, along with the dignitaries, departed the hotel. It was time for all the events of the day.

The first stop was the site of the monument to the Sixth New Jersey Regiment, down near Devil's Den. That ceremony began what to John promised to be an ordeal. The ceremony dedicating that memorial also marked the start of the dedications of all the other New Jersey monuments as well as speeches by the prominent dignitaries. Those dignitaries included Robert S. Green, the Governor of New Jersey, and the Adjutant General of the state, William S. Stryker.

There were pauses throughout as the participants moved to the locations of the monuments on the field to the Eighth and the Seventh New Jersey regiments, along with Clark's Battery B.

After that, the large throng headed to the Eleventh New Jersey's memorial, located just south of the Klingel house. The fence rails near that location had been removed so people could gather in close to hear the speeches. Colonel James N. Duffy, the head of the New Jersey Gettysburg Battlefield Commission, spoke a few words in which he introduced Schoonover to the assembled throng. Already weary from all the other events of the day, he unfolded himself from his seat. The warmth of the late June day, his health, and the emotions of the moment hammered at him. He looked out over the crowd, seeing faces of those he recognized from their service together. That gave him strength. He cleared his throat and began. As he started his speech, he thought to himself, *I hope and pray this does justice to the sacrifice here…and to General McAllister.*

"Your Excellency Governor Green and Surviving Comrades: I rejoice with you to-day that so many of us, after the lapse of a quarter of a century, have been permitted to assemble upon this historic field to participate in the dedication of this beautiful monument erected by our State, not only to commemorate the valor and the patriotism of those who died in their country's defense, but to aid in impressing upon the minds of the living the fearful cost of maintaining its unity." He paused, longing for a cool drink of water, licked his dry lips, and then pressed on.

"The Eleventh Regiment, New Jersey Volunteers, left Trenton [on] August twenty-fifth, 1862, and reported at Washington the following day. It remained near Alexandria, Virginia, and performed various camp duties until the sixteenth day of November, when it was attached to the brigade of General Carr, Sickles' division, and entered upon active duty with the Army of the Potomac.

"Neither the time nor the location proved favorable to the health of the men, and when the regiment took up its march for Fredericksburg four commissioned officers and two-hundred-and-fifteen enlisted men were left behind upon the sick list.

"Our first experience under fire was at Fredericksburg, with Burnside, and cost us two men killed and five wounded. When the Eleventh Regiment left for the field, it was followed by no prophecies of a brilliant future—in fact, it was often spoken of as a regiment of boys; but the opportunity soon arrived which enabled them to prove that though age and stature might be wanting, they possessed qualities which amply compensated for both."

He took a deep breath, pushing down the emotions now welling up inside him, and continued.

"The Regiment went into the battle of Chancellorsville with five-hundred men and sustained a loss of one-hundred-and-ninety-two. Two officers and thirty-three enlisted men were killed; nineteen were left dead upon the field of battle and twelve died of wounds a short time after. Sickness near Alexandria and the heavy losses in the battle of Chancellorsville had so decimated our ranks, that when we reached the battlefield of Gettysburg, we numbered but two-hundred-and-seventy-five men.

"Near the spot upon which we now stand the regiment took up its position on that eventful afternoon of July second, 1863. About 3 o'clock the enemy opened with artillery. For an hour or more the earth trembled with the jar of guns, and tons of metal were hurled over and fell around us. At this time our right was resting just in rear of the Smith house, over there, the line extending down through the orchard, the left being under the brow of the hill.[3]

"Major Kearny, who was standing near me on the left of the regiment excitedly exclaimed: 'We are going to have a fight.' A moment later he was mortally wounded and carried to the rear. We were now receiving a fire from Wilcox's brigade from beyond the Emmitsburg pike, and from Barksdale's brigade, which was advancing in full view just down by the road which leads to Little Round Top.

"I then passed rapidly to the right of the regiment to notify the Colonel of the absence of the Major, and learned that he, too, had been wounded and taken to the rear. Captain Martin, the senior officer present, was then notified that he was in command of the regiment. At this time an order was received from General Carr to slightly change the front by bringing the left to the rear. This was to check the advance of Barksdale's brigade, now in full view in the field beyond.

---

[3] Although Schoonover cites the house around which the Eleventh fought on July 2, 1863 as the Smith house in his dedication speech, at the time of the battle it was known as the Klingel house.

"This movement being executed, the entire regiment opened an effective fire upon the advancing line of the enemy. At this point, word was conveyed to me that both Captains Martin and Logan were wounded and being carried to the rear. A moment later and Captain Ackerman fell dead by my side. The two former were killed before they reached a place of safety.

"Barksdale, mounted on a spirited horse, was now riding some distance in advance of his brigade, waving his sword, and urging his men forward. An order was received from General Carr to 'bring down that mounted officer.' Captain Cory, who is with us to-day, commanded the company on the extreme left of the regiment, and the execution of the order was committed to him and his command. Barksdale fell, and the Rebel army did not have among its losses a braver man than he who on July second, 1863, led his brigade in their gallant charge down through these fields to our left.

"The fire of the enemy at this time was perfectly terrific; men were falling on every side. Slowly and stubbornly the regiment fell back, keeping up a continuous fire.

"Two color-bearers had been shot down, and as a last effort to rally what remained of the regiment, Corporal Johnson was ordered to take the colors, plant them twenty yards to the front, and not to leave his position without orders. Amidst the confusion and retreat, he was almost forgotten. I hastened back, and Johnson was still there, with his guard standing like statues amidst the shower of shot and shell falling around them.

"But how fared the regiment all this time? Lines cut in imperishable granite, upon the monument which marks this sacred spot, is the record which it submits to posterity, of the part it took to stem the advancing tide of rebellion on the afternoon of July second, 1863. Out of two-hundred-and-seventy-five men taken into the fight, one-hundred-and-fifty-two had fallen, including every commissioned officer above the rank of Lieutenant."

His lips were now quivering; the emotions resurfaced by the day itself, the sorrow, the heavy grief of the loss of so many comrades swirling in his mind, the illness of his beloved General McAllister —

all of it now pressed in on him. With another deep breath and another licking of his parched lips, he willed himself to finish. He was almost done.

"My time is too limited to give you a detailed history of our organization, but I wish to say that the regiment took part in all the subsequent battles of the Army of the Potomac. Its losses were heavy at Spotsylvania—Captain Sleeper, Adjutant Baldwin, and Lieutenant Egan being among the killed. Forty fell at Locust Grove, and at the first attack upon Petersburg, where Captain Layton fell, we lost forty-four."

Almost done. *Dear God,* he thought, *please help me!* He felt a hand grasp his. His beloved Lizzie looked up at him and squeezed his hand to encourage him.

"New Jersey may well be proud of the record which her soldiers made in the War of the Rebellion, and as a member of the Eleventh Regiment, New Jersey Volunteers, one who was with it from the time it first set foot upon Virginia soil until the final close at Appomattox, I do not hesitate to say that it bore well its part in the grandest army that ever struck for liberty, nationality, and the rights of man."[4]

With that, he was finished. All that remained was the actual dedication of the monument. Gathering himself again, the tears mingling with his sweat, he shuffled back to his seat, and sat down.

After the dedication of the Eleventh's monument, the throng then proceeded to the west side of the Emmitsburg Road just south of the Rogers House. At that site, the monument to the Fifth New Jersey was dedicated. Its surviving colonel, William J. Sewell, delivered a few remarks filled with passionate thoughts of remembrance, and dedication.

For Schoonover, the remainder of the day sped by in a blur. It was then on to the Bryan farm, to inspect the memorial to the Twelfth New Jersey, which had previously been dedicated the year before. The final ceremony of the day was that of the First New Jersey Brigade's monument. At the First New Jersey Brigade's location,

---

[4] Quoted practically verbatim from Schoonover's speech as noted in the *Final Report of the Gettysburg Battle-Field Commission of New Jersey,* pp. 54-56.

representatives from each of the regiments that made up the brigade spoke. At the conclusion of all the addresses and speeches transferring all the New Jersey monuments dedicated this day to Governor James A. Beaver of Pennsylvania and president of the Gettysburg Battlefield Memorial Association, John's ordeal was over. Exhausted, he was haunted by the remembrance of all the men whose faces who flashed before him.

The carriage ride back to the hotel seemed to pass very quickly. *Thank God it's done; it's done,* he thought to himself. Lizzie again squeezed his hand and kissed his cheek. "I love you John, *Colonel* John." A deep smile, eyes dancing, creased her beautiful face.

"Thank you," John replied to his wife.

"Well done, my dear husband. *Well done!* If he could be here, the General would be *so* proud of you!"

February 23, 1891

Hotel Belvidere,

Belvidere, New Jersey

Robert McAllister alternated between sleep and being awake, and also murmuring commands, Bible verses, and hymns. Outside, the snow had been gently falling for a while now. Its white covering turned everything into the freshness that comes with a new snowfall. The snow helped transform this bleak, gray day into a day of pure blessing, wiping away the barren winter ugliness.

Standing next to the window of the room in which her husband lay, Ellen McAllister sighed that deep sigh of pending grief and yes, even resignation. Not well herself, she shuddered at that sense of grief and at the steadily growing relief that Robert's suffering would soon be over. Ellen barely left his side during these final hours of life. The family had gathered. Their two daughters, along with their husbands, and some of the adult grandchildren, alternated with each other on this final watch. Ellen McAllister looked over at her beloved husband, covered in several layers of blankets and his favorite comforter. As it struggled against the winter chill, the snap and pop of the steam radiator in the corner broke the silence in the small room.

There was a knock on the door. When Ellen answered it, John and Lizzie Schoonover walked into the room. Behind them was John's cousin Amos, who'd also served on McAllister's staff during the war. "The Colonel," or Colonel John, as Schoonover had come to be known on the other side of the Delaware River, held a top hat in his hand. The overcoats of both men still bore traces of the falling snow. John's full face, covered under the mutton chops he'd worn for a long time plus the gray streaks in his hair, indicated the passing of the years since the end of the "War of Rebellion" — as Robert was so often heard to quote.

Lizzie Schoonover took Ellen's hand in her own, and said, "It is good to see you again, my dear! Though not under these circumstances!"

Ellen nodded and wiped away a tear, grateful at Lizzie's kind words of commiseration. She took John's and Amos's overcoats and hats, and carefully placed them on a chair in a corner of the room. Lizzie Schoonover shrugged out of her own winter coat and positioned it over the chair as well.

Looking down at the form of his beloved commander and dear friend, John softly asked, "Mrs. McAllister, how is he?"

Ellen responded, "The doctor just left; it will not be long now. He is fading rapidly." *Oh my,* she thought to herself. *He doesn't deserve to go like this!* She remembered how his health slowly receded, first from the diabetes, then the stroke, and now the kidney failure (or "Bright's disease" as the doctor said). But she also recalled how Robert repeatedly told her he wanted no military trappings at his funeral. *In another way,* she thought to herself, *it would have been better if he had died in battle.*

Almost as if Schoonover read her mind, he chimed in with that very thought. "Mrs. McAllister, as we have watched him fade away over the years, I think he would have been better off had he died in battle."

McAllister's face—which had a pale, almost ashen hue to it—was not the face of the man John remembered. At that moment, Robert uttered orders from some long-ago battle. "Come on, men! Close up; close up!" In delirium, he muttered, "Hold fast there; hold fast! John! Schoonover, you *must* take command!"

Tears trickling down his face, Schoonover came over to the side of the bed. "General, sir; I am here! What are your orders, sir? I am *here,* sir!" McAllister's eyes fluttered at the sound of Schoonover's voice, and the limp side of his face quivered. A tear mingled with the drool from the corner of his mouth, forming a small rivulet. Schoonover removed a handkerchief from his pocket, ever so gently wiping the mingled moisture from the side of his colonel's face.

Witnessing this scene, Ellen went to her daughters, wrapping her arms around them both. All three had tears running down their cheeks in mutual mourning. Even Lizzie was softly crying.

Time passed in the sad vigil. Suddenly, McAllister's eyes flashed open. Then he began mumbling. Ellen went to him. At first she could not make it out. *Something about a hymn, but which one?* Robert struggled to say something. She leaned in closer. In a whisper, he said, "Amazing…Grace." She looked at him, unsure of his meaning. "Sing…Amazing…Grace," he whispered. "Last verse," he said quietly, "last verse." Ellen looked at her children and then back at Robert. Tears rolling down her cheeks, she began to gently sing the last verse of that beloved old hymn: "When we've been there ten thousand years, bright shining as the sun…" First her daughters and their husbands joined in; then the adult grandchildren present; and finally John and Amos Schoonover and John's wife Lizzie. The harmonies of the old hymn filled the room.

For the briefest of moments, Robert's face was normal again. He sang with them all now, with every last ounce of strength he still possessed: "To sing God's praise, than when we first begun!" For an instant, that rich baritone voice whose lion-like roar had thundered over so many battlefields, joined in on the chorus.

When they finished the last line, McAllister's strong hand grabbed that of his beloved wife. He smiled at his assembled family, tears running down his cheeks. His eyes then showed his recognition of John and Lizzie Schoonover, and next Amos Schoonover. He weakly nodded his head. "Yes, yes," he whispered. "We… shall…see…each…other…again!" A heavy sigh followed. Then silence…and he was gone.

March 5, 1891
Belvidere, New Jersey

Brevet Major General Robert McAllister's funeral service had just concluded. It was time to leave the church. Heavy with grief, Schoonover knew he had to convey a presence of calmness amid the storm of this incredible sense of loss. *Steady, John,* he thought to himself. *Steady. You* have *to do this for Mrs. McAllister and the girls and their families.*

As the coffin, draped in the tattered flag of the old Third Corps, was slowly brought down the aisle from where it stood in the front of the sanctuary, he fell in with the rest of the honorary pallbearers. They followed behind Ellen McAllister, the daughters, their husbands, and a sizable contingent of the grandchildren. The rest of those in attendance began their preparations to exit as well.

For a second time that morning, the church organ burst into McAllister's beloved hymn of "Amazing Grace." This was more in triumph than in mourning. John's mind flashed back to the first time he'd heard it in camp. He almost managed a smile at the memory of that day so long ago, then quickly suppressed it.

The procession paused briefly at the doors to the church. The doors opened and the last phrases of the hymn thundered out, like a clap of thunder. The pallbearers, which included John and selected representatives of the male grandchildren, carefully lifted the coffin to carry it to the waiting caisson. Replaced on the coffin by a national flag, the old Third Corps guidon was quickly attached to a flagstaff.

At first, John didn't notice them. But there they were. Hundreds of people were gathered in the street and in the park nearby. A murmur spread through the crowd as it saw the caisson with the coffin on it. To honor its favorite son at his passing all the businesses, both county and municipal offices, and all the schools shut down for this day. Then the procession started off. A small band started the funeral cadence, with the *drrrr drumppp drumppp* of the drums setting the tone.

As the procession wound its way toward the cemetery, John saw the streets were lined with townspeople. All the men stood with heads uncovered; some of the ladies were even dressed in black. Flags draped with black crepe marked every corner. Grown men and women, some children even, were openly weeping. Or at least dabbing their eyes.

Thomas D. Marbaker, one of the many survivors of the Eleventh Regiment and also its historian, carried the old corps guidon. Leading the procession, he walked straight as a ramrod with steady, measured steps. But even he, too, from time and time brushed tears from his face with his white gloved hands.

John Schoonover looked at the men around him. Joseph Carr, the brigade commander of the Eleventh from the time it began its service; William Stryker, the Adjutant General of the State of New Jersey; William Sewell, the Colonel of the Fifth New Jersey whom McAllister at one time called a drunkard and a coward. Sewell and McAllister had long ago settled their differences. Now he was a pallbearer, at Ellen McAllister's urgent pleading and request. Even Stephen Moore, the Eleventh's original Lieutenant Colonel, was there to honor his former commanding officer.

Along the way, John also noticed the old soldiers, marked with the G.A.R. medallion. All wore some link back to that historic time of their service. A piece of a uniform here; a kepi there; treasured corps badges. All told the story of young men thinking it more important to preserve the Union; to maintain and uphold the Constitution; to lay their young lives on the sacred altar of freedom as McAllister had once called it.

The drums rolled on; a small band leading, alternating between hymns, a strung-out version of *Frog in the Well* – the Eleventh's old "fighting song" as they went into battle, and patriotic tunes. As they marched, the crowd of townspeople closed in behind them, swelling the size of the procession.

Finally, the cemetery came into view. The procession made the left-hand turn in; the riderless horse with reversed boots in the stirrup leading. At last, they came to the grave where their beloved general would be laid to rest. The throng circled to the left to an open area where a platform had been hastily built.

The caisson bearing McAllister's casket halted next to the grave. Schoonover and the pallbearers stepped up to the caisson's rear, lining up to receive the coffin. Intermingled to help were some of McAllister's younger adult grandchildren. Hand over hand they pulled the casket from the caisson and lifted it to their collective shoulders. Carefully they stepped to the open grave. Slowly and reverently, they lowered the coffin to the supports over it. And then, under Schoonover's commands, they marched to the waiting platform that had been set up. Once Schoonover and the rest of the pallbearers joined the assembled family, the Reverend E. Clarke Cline, pastor of the Westminster Presbyterian Church in Phillipsburg, New Jersey, and former regimental chaplain, stepped forward to begin the graveside service.

April 12, 1930
Stroudsburg, Pennsylvania

The warm mid-day sun filled the solarium of the hospital as John's son Frank wheeled him out. The sounds of the town, honking of horns, whistles of police, the steady murmur of it all, the daily buzz of life, greeted him. The first robin of spring alighted itself on the railing of the porch not far from where the wheelchair had stopped.

His son took the blanket he had brought with him, and carefully covered his father's legs with it. John patted his son's hands, as a way of saying "thank you."

"Would you like some tea, Father?" Frank said.

"Yes, son," John replied. "That would be very nice."

"Then I shall go at once, Father, to see to it for you." And Frank left.

John settled in to enjoy this day. He found himself thinking, *How many more days will I get to see like this?* He coughed, and then sighed. *Blasted pneumonia. Just keeps hanging on,* he thought.

He also remembered, as he often did, his beloved Lizzie (or Elizabeth) who had passed away ten years before. In his twilight years, he now cherished the long life they had together and the memories they had created. He missed her so much. *Oh, what a wonderful woman you were, Lizzie,* he thought to himself. *You were so good to me. And I miss you so much…So much…*

The warmth of the sun, accentuated by the solarium, made him sleepy. He shifted as he wanted to stay awake to enjoy this day, but he was also so tired, *so tired.* He fell into a warm, dreamy doze.

Out of the warm glow, what looked like a face appeared slowly. At first, he couldn't see it clearly. Slowly and surely it came into focus. "John," the voice softly called him. "John Schoonover…"

"How are you, my dearest!" Schoonover murmured.

"Oh, John, I have missed you so…" It was Lizzie.

John said, "I have missed you, too, my dear! So much! So much…"

Lizzie held out a hand. "John, I want to go for a walk, down by the stream. Will you come?"

"Oh, my dear Lizzie," he mumbled, "Oh, yes! Let's do so!"

He grabbed her hand, and they came to a bridge over the stream.

"John," she said to him, "let's cross over!"

"My dear Lizzie," he mumbled. "Are you sure it's safe?"

"Yes, John," she said. "There are friends there as well; *good* friends. They are all waiting for us."

Slowly but surely out of the mist came the faces of friends. First to greet him was Jesus himself, the very one who had made this all a surety! Next was Robert McAllister, his beloved regimental colonel and then brigade commander; with him was his dear wife Ellen. Led by McAllister, the small band approached an open clearing. Suddenly the Long Roll sounded on the drums and *Officer's Call* reverberated on the bugle. Before them, a long line of tents appeared, set up in their customary organized layout, all in perfection. Then, lined up in order by company, was the entire Eleventh New Jersey. Whole and complete again, with the national and state colors snapping ever so lightly in the breeze.

When he saw them all, John's joy was complete. All his brother officers, including Philip Kearny, Andrew Ackerman, Dorastus Logan, Samuel Sleeper, and Luther Martin, were there. Even privates like Jake Mount, Joseph Cheston, and Billy Fraley—who were grinning from ear to ear. And surprisingly, his cousin Amos was there too! He thought to himself, *They are all here! They are* all *here!!*

As one, the regiment snapped to attention. The enlisted men and the officers came to *"Present, Arms."* Yes, it was perfect. As it should be; as it should be. John heard McAllister's deep baritone voice, "Welcome home, John! *Welcome home!"*

Frank Schoonover came through the doors with his father's favorite tea. Right away, he noticed a smile on his father's face. His eyes were closed; there was such a peaceful look on it. Frank set the tray down on a small table and went to him. "Father," he said, shaking him ever so gently. "Father!" One more time, he lightly shook him. "Father!" He felt his father's wrist; there was no pulse. The tears flowed down his cheeks. "Ohhhh, Father!!!! Oh, please, don't go!"

Drying his tears, Frank realized where his father was. He'd crossed over the river, to where he'd longed to go for so many, many years. Yes, the prayers had been answered. His father, John Schoonover of the Eleventh New Jersey—the "good Colonel," Colonel John, the Patriarch of Bushkill Falls—had gone finally home.

Whatever Happened To?

Robert McAllister

McAllister recovers from his wounds and returns to the Eleventh New Jersey in early October of 1863. Though still weak, he resumes command of the regiment for a brief period. Promoted to Brevet Brigadier General, the Second New Jersey Brigade is entrusted to him. It includes the Fifth, Sixth, Seventh, Eighth, and Eleventh New Jersey Regiments, and also the One-Hundred-and-Fifteenth Pennsylvania. Several of these regiments are later reduced officially to battalions. He is wounded twice more (though minor), and serves out the war. He attains the brevet rank of Major General in March of 1865. At the war's conclusion he declines the Army's request that he stay in. He returns to civilian life and the railroad company he'd left back in 1861. Active in events of the Grand Army of the Republic (G.A.R.) and reunions, McAllister makes it a point to share the Gospel of Jesus Christ at every reunion.

In the early 1870s, he and his family move to Allentown, Pennsylvania, to be closer to his job as General Manager of the Ironton Company (specializing in railroad construction) and the Trenton Railroad. Robert and Ellen purchase a burial plot in a cemetery in that town. Also while in Allentown, the Governor of Pennsylvania appoints McAllister to a commission to research the establishment of a Soldiers' Home for veterans with mental health issues. His health begins to fail in the late 1870s. The toll of old battle wounds, age, and Bright's disease make it harder for him to work.

McAllister and his partner Robert Kennedy dissolve the Ironton Company in 1882. Kennedy insists that McAllister move to his estate in Belvidere. Until his former partner's sudden death in 1887, he resides at the old Erlanbach estate. McAllister then has to move into the Hotel Belvidere and take up residence. Shortly before the dedication of the monument at Gettysburg to the Eleventh New Jersey in 1888, he suffers a stroke which leaves him weak and destitute. McAllister dies in the hotel in 1891, a broken man both physically and financially. Because the town fathers insist on it, his wife Ellen buries him in the cemetery in Belvidere. He repeatedly tells his wife he wants *no* military trappings at his funeral. Nevertheless, he gets just that.

Lieutenant Colonel Stephen J. Moore

His service record notes that at the battle of Chancellorsville, his horse was shot out from under him. Knocked unconscious from his horse falling on him and from heatstroke, he temporarily re-joins the regiment on July 27, 1863. However, he resigns his position and never again sees active service with the Eleventh. In the fall of 1863, Moore joins the Sixteenth Regiment, Veteran Reserve Corps, and is given command of the Sherburne Barracks in Washington, D.C. In January of 1864, he is sent to the prison camp at Elmira, New York to serve as President of a Courts-Martial Board. In October of that same year, he is given command over all the guards at the Elmira prison camp. He serves in that capacity until the end of the war. A native of New Brunswick, New Jersey, he lives until August 29, 1901. He is buried in the Willow Grove cemetery in his birthplace.

John Schoonover

According to Marbaker's history of the Eleventh, Adjutant Schoonover is slightly wounded on July 2 at Gettysburg. Temporarily in command of the regiment on July 3, his horse is shot out from under him during the famous cannonade preceding Pickett's Charge. On August 21, 1863 Schoonover receives a richly deserved promotion to Lt. Colonel; he then takes full command of the regiment. Shortly before the close of the war he receives a Brevet Colonelcy. He commands the regiment much the way McAllister did—with a steady, solid hand. As noted, he survives the war and returns to his beloved Oxford, New Jersey home and employment in the Oxford Iron Works. He then moves to Trenton, New Jersey, where he ends up selling insurance. Among his clients are Mr. and Mrs. Washington and Emily Roebling, builders of the Brooklyn Bridge and owners of the Roebling Steel works. John and his beloved wife Elizabeth (or Lizzie as he calls her) have two sons: Frank and John Depue. Frank survives to adulthood and becomes an incredibly famous artist in Wilmington, Delaware.

Post-war, his veteran pension application describes medical conditions of liver issues, dysentery, and "the piles." These ailments stay with him until his death. Post-Civil War, Schoonover becomes very prominent in veterans' affairs, attending every reunion of the regiment. He continues his close relationship with McAllister till the latter's passing in 1891.

Schoonover delivers the dedication speech for the regimental monument at Gettysburg in 1888, as well as for McAllister's memorial in the cemetery at Belvidere, New Jersey, on Memorial Day, 1893.

When he retires, he returns to his beloved Bushkill Falls. There he comes to be known not only as "Colonel John," but also the patriarch of his town. Schoonover outlives his wife, dying in 1930. At his viewing, for four hours people will stand and wait their turn to pay their respects in a pouring rain. He is among the last of New Jersey's surviving Civil War veterans.

First Lieutenant William J. Mount, Co. A

Mount becomes the Eleventh's first regimental Sergeant Major on September 1, 1862. He previously served in the Third Regiment, New Jersey Militia, with Stephen Moore, the Eleventh's original Lieutenant Colonel. Mount then also serves with McAllister and Schoonover in the First New Jersey Regiment. In April of 1863, he is promoted to First Lieutenant, Co. A. Unlike so many others of the regiment, he survives Gettysburg unscathed. But Gettysburg appears to be his undoing.

Fourteen days later, during an action of the Third Corps with a rear-guard of the Army of Northern Virginia at Manassas Gap (Wapping Heights) on July 23, 1863, the Eleventh was drawn up in line of battle. During that action, an incident occurred that resulted in the dishonorable dismissal from the service of the United States, *without a trial,* of a lieutenant in command of his company. During that skirmish, there was an officer who says he would not go into the fight because he would "disgrace himself and his company." Schoonover, who had taken command, sought to make an example of this officer. He sent a letter to the commanding general of the Army of the Potomac asking this officer be removed for cowardice in the face of the enemy. On July 24, 1863, that lieutenant was so dismissed, by command of Major General Meade.

William Stryker's *Record of Officers and Men from New Jersey in the Civil War, 1861-1865* notes that Mount was dismissed via Special Order 129, paragraph 46, War Department, Adjutant General Office, Washington, D.C. dated May 6, 1864. That order *specifically* references the events of July 23, 1863. It is noted in the Adjutant General's official records that Mount tries three times to get his pension. But he is denied due to his dishonorable discharge for cowardice "in the face of the enemy."[5]

---

[5] *Marbaker,* p. 117; *N.J. Civil War Record,* p. 543; *Eleventh New Jersey Regimental Records,* New Jersey State Archives.

He and his brother buy property in 1876 in Freehold, New Jersey. He then sells the property to his brother in 1878. There is a William Mount who appears in the census in the 1880s who is living in Salt Lake City, Utah. The authors haven't been able to confirm if it's him or not. The birth year matches his age when he musters into the Eleventh New Jersey. Other than that, he disappears into history.

Commissary Sergeant Philip D. Crisp

He musters in with the regiment and does a great job as Commissary Sergeant. He remains in that rank until he is promoted after the war to First Lieutenant, Co. G, on June 13, 1865. That action occurs after the regiment musters out of service on June 6, 1865. It is the authors' opinion that this took place for pension purposes and a "thank you for a job well done." After the war, he returns to private life as a carriage maker in Trenton, New Jersey. He dies in that city on April 14, 1899 at the age of fifty-six.

Major Philip Kearny

Kearny is promoted to Major following the resignation of Valentine Mutchler on April 4, 1863. He serves in that rank during the battles of Chancellorsville and Gettysburg. Following his wounding at the Klingel farm, he is carried to the rear and placed in the same tent as McAllister. Kearny rallies for a bit from his leg wound but loses said leg in the resulting treatment. Subsequently transported to St. Luke's (U. S. Army Gen. Hosp.) Hospital in his home city of New York, he dies there from pneumonia and a blood clot on August 9, 1863. He is then buried in the family plot in the New York suburbs. Letters that he wrote home to his family are posthumously published post-war. They are extremely critical of McAllister's commanding of the regiment, insisting he could have done better. In a letter to the editor, McAllister's reply is basically that he will not criticize a dead man's honor or position. Rather, he does note that under his command, Kearny had proven to be a very capable, courageous, and excellent leader of men. The controversy fades into history. Shortly after his death, Kearny is brevetted to Lt. Colonel, and then Colonel.

Surgeon Edward L. Welling

For his work at Chancellorsville and Gettysburg, Welling is promoted to command of the Third Corps medical and hospital staffs. When the Third Corps is merged into the Second Corps during the March 1864 reorganization of the Army of the Potomac, he takes over the command of the Second Corps medical staff. He turns that command into a model for the rest of the army's medical service. He eventually finds himself in command of the Army of the Potomac's medical staff, including all the surgeons. He survives the war and goes on to have a long life as a doctor. He dies on November 29, 1897 and is buried in the cemetery in Pennington, New Jersey.

Sergeant Major Henry C. Tilton

He is promoted from Sergeant, Co. C, to Sgt. Major on April 14, 1863. He then receives promotion to First Lieutenant, Company B, on November 13, 1863. He serves at that rank until war's end and the mustering out of the regiment. He also fades back into history. He dies on December 26, 1930 at age ninety. Buried in the Easton, Pennsylvania cemetery, his headstone reads "First Lieutenant, Eleventh New Jersey."

Captain John J. Willis, Company C

Willis musters in with the Regiment. He is gone by the Spring of 1863, as he resigns due to disability. Fading into history, he dies on February 14, 1891. He is buried in Mercer Cemetery, in Trenton, New Jersey.

Captain Andrew H. Ackerman, Co. C

His body is recovered and is first interred on the field by the Klingel barn. His remains are then exhumed and returned to New Jersey to be buried in the family plot in an old Dutch Reformed cemetery in Jersey City, New Jersey. When that falls into disrepair, his remains are moved to another in Totowa, New Jersey. When his second burial falls into a state of ruin, information on where his remains are subsequently moved is lost. Much speculation and research by both the late Bob McAvoy and author Jim Lamason suggests that his remains either now lie under a parking garage for a hospital or in a mass grave in another cemetery. As this book is published, the search continues.

Second Lieutenant John B. Faussett, Co. C

He is seriously wounded at Gettysburg. He survives, recovers, and soldiers on with the regiment until the spring of 1864, when he is struck down by heatstroke. He musters out on July 19, 1864 for disability. Dying on March 8, 1899, he is also buried at Mercer Cemetery in Trenton, New Jersey.

Private Joseph Cheston, Co. C

His remains are buried on the field, most likely by the Klingel barn. His family is poor, so they cannot pay to have his body returned to them for proper burial near home. During McAllister's recovery, there is a service held in Trenton in Cheston's memory. He now lies either near the barn in an unmarked grave or is numbered among the many graves in the Soldiers' National Cemetery at Gettysburg that are marked "Unknown" in either the New Jersey section or the general Unknown section.

Captain Samuel T. Sleeper, Co. I

As noted in the story, he is emotionally and physically beat up at Gettysburg. He does recover and remains in command of his company. As Schoonover notes in his speech dedicating the memorial to the Eleventh at Gettysburg, Sleeper is killed during the grand assault by the Second Corps (of which the Eleventh New Jersey had become part) against the "Mule Shoe" salient of the Army of Northern Virginia's position at Spotsylvania Court House on May 12, 1864. Buried by his fellow officers on the battlefield, the present location of his remains is unknown.

Major General Daniel E. Sickles

He famously loses a leg on July 2 at Gettysburg from a shell fired by Confederate artillery, which causes him to leave the Army of the Potomac. The first one back to Washington D.C., and visited by Lincoln shortly after his return, Sickles insists it is *he* who caused Meade to stay and fight. Though he tries to return to the army, he never again serves with the Army of the Potomac. Sickles lives on until 1914. Before his death, he participates in many visits to the old Gettysburg battlefield as well as veteran reunions. He even becomes fast friends with his old Confederate opponent, Lt. General James Longstreet. When asked where his monument is on the battlefield, he barks that "the whole damn field" is his monument. It is he who initiates the movement to preserve the battlefield for posterity. A portrait bust of Sickles was planned to be included with the Excelsior Brigade monument at Gettysburg but was never completed. This was due to Sickles losing his job as Park Commissioner because of charges of embezzlement.

Major General G. Gordon Meade

Meade survives Gettysburg and is proclaimed as the victor. He learns that the President is unhappy with him, as Lincoln thinks he did not aggressively pursue Lee and the Army of Northern Virginia. Recent scholarship and research by many authors have shown the Army of the Potomac was so badly hurt, that while it did pursue Lee's retreating Army of Northern Virginia with cavalry and infantry, it was with much difficulty. Under Lt. General Ulysses Grant, Meade serves as the Army of the Potomac's commander to the end of the war. He dies in 1872 and is buried in the family plot in Laurel Hill Cemetery in Philadelphia, Pennsylvania. Meade is not just remembered for being the Victor of Gettysburg. He is also responsible for a number of lighthouses built along the East Coast of the United States in the decades before the Civil War. The lighthouses at Cape May, New Jersey, and Long Beach Island, New Jersey, are two of his lighthouses.

The Third Corps, Army of the Potomac

With the heavy losses suffered during the battles of Chancellorsville and Gettysburg and the need to reorganize the leadership of the Army of the Potomac, the Third Corps gets merged into the Second Corps in March of 1864. Many of the common soldiers, and even men like McAllister (who incorporates the old Third Corps emblem with the Second Corps emblem in his brigade flag), voice their displeasure through various means at the disbanding of their old Third Corps. (McAllister's brigade flag is pictured on the back cover of this book. It is also draped over his coffin and carried in front of it in the procession to the cemetery for his burial.)

The Flags

The original state flag is replaced by another one, this time with the state symbol. The battle-scarred national flag is retired and replaced with another flag. McAllister's family donates his brigade flag to the state of New Jersey for safe keeping. The regimental stand of colors, along with the brigade flag, is now part of the New Jersey Civil War flag display that can be seen in the New Jersey State Museum in Trenton, New Jersey. (The flags may be seen on the back cover.)

The Eleventh Regiment, New Jersey Volunteer Infantry

Regimental historian Thomas Marbaker writes of the regiment being placed in a reserve position "in a rocky woodland" on the morning of July 3, 1863 at Gettysburg. Marbaker notes, "a ration of hard bread and coffee was issued in the morning, and somewhat later in the day a ration of fresh meat was brought up, but before it could be issued, orders came to fall in. Leaving a guard over the meat—for that was too precious to lose—we started on a double-quick to the right and front. After proceeding nearly a mile, a halt was made in rear of a line of batteries, which occupied the crest in front. This position was held during the heavy cannonading that preceded Pickett's Charge, and until the charge had been repulsed. Then we marched back to our former position...."[6]

In a review of the surgeon's report, almost every surviving member is hurt or wounded in some manner. After the battle, the regiment will have its rosters filled out with draftees and some volunteers. It acquits itself well under Schoonover's command, fighting during the battle of Locust Hill, Bristoe Station, into the Wilderness and through the Overland Campaign under Grant. It is with the Army of the Potomac at the surrender at Appomattox. It will change chaplains during that time to the Rev. E. Clarke Cline. However, it will never really be truly the same again. The battles of Chancellorsville, and then Gettysburg, gutted its core and tore the heart out of it. The regiment will also have the unenviable distinction of having one of the highest desertion rates from late 1863 to the end of the war and its being mustered out.

Reverend E. Clarke Cline

Mustering in as a regimental chaplain after Gettysburg on September 11, 1863, Cline will play a major role in getting the regiment back together. He has some experience as a pastor of a church in Doe Run, Pennsylvania. He meets daily with McAllister, and then Schoonover, and with the officers and men of the unit. When the regiment goes into battle, he is at the front to give aid and comfort to the wounded and dying. At war's end, he becomes pastor of a

6 *Marbaker*, p. 101.

Presbyterian church in Oxford, New Jersey. In 1886, he takes over as pastor of the Westminster Presbyterian Church in Phillipsburg, New Jersey. He will have a stained-glass window installed there in memory of the officers and men of the Eleventh. (On the back cover of this book is a photo of that window, which just a few years ago was restored and re-dedicated.) He retires as pastor from that church in 1901. He dies on August 20, 1916. He is buried in a family plot in a cemetery in Easton, Pennsylvania.

Photos of
Key Personalities

Major General
George Gordon Meade,
Commanding General,
Army of the Potomac

Major General
Daniel E. Sickles,
Commander,
III Army Corps,
Army of the Potomac

Brigadier General
Alexander A. Humphreys,
Second Division,
III Army Corps,
Army of the Potomac

Brigadier General
Joseph Carr,
1st Brigade, 2nd Division,
III Army Corps,
Army of the Potomac

Colonel
Robert McAllister,
Eleventh Regiment, NJVI
(taken while recovering
From Gettysburg wounds)

Lieutenant Colonel
Stephen J. Moore,
Eleventh Regiment, NJVI
(absent, recovering from
Chancellorsville injuries)

Major
Philip Kearny,
Eleventh Regiment, NJVI
(nephew of Major General
Philip Kearny, killed at
Chantilly, Va.,
August, 1862)

Surgeon (Major)
Edward L. Welling,
Eleventh Regiment, NJVI

First Lieutenant and Adjutant
John Schoonover,
Eleventh Regiment, NJVI
(promoted to
Lieutenant Colonel,
August 21, 1863)

Captain
Andrew H. Ackerman,
Co. C, Eleventh Regiment,
NJVI
(killed at Gettysburg)

First Lieutenant
William J. Mount,
Co. A, Eleventh Regiment,
NJVI
(Author Jim Lamason's
Relative)

Second Lieutenant
John B. Faussett,
Co. C, Eleventh Regiment,
NJVI

Captain
Luther Martin,
Co. D, Eleventh Regiment,
NJVI

Captain
Wm. H. Lloyd,
Co. F, Eleventh Regiment,
NJVI

Captain
Dorastus Logan,
Co. H, Eleventh Regiment,
NJVI

Captain
Samuel T. Sleeper,
Co. I, Eleventh Regiment,
NJVI

List of Names of Casualties Suffered by the Eleventh Regiment at Gettysburg, July 2–3, 1863[7]

Killed in Action:

Company C:
Captain Andrew Ackerman; Sergeant Corum Richter; Privates Joseph Cheston, John Clark.

Company D:
Captain Luther Martin; Corporal Isaac Hendershot; Private Randolph Merriman.

Company E:
Private Thomas Tinney.

Company F:
Private John L. Cozzins.

Company G:
Privates George S. Bird, George H. Bunting, Henry Elbertson, Michael Goff, Stewart Parent, and Peter Robbins.

---

[7] *Marbaker*, pp. 106–107; *N.J. Civil War Record*, pp. 542–583.

Company H:

Captain Dorastus B. Logan; Private Edward Barber.

Company K:

Corporals Wm. H. Morgan, Jeremiah O'Brien; Privates Henry Kring, Martin Bekie.

Missing in Action:

Company D:

Privates James Beatty (recorded at War Dept., July 2, 1863; as died that date), Frederick C. Tuers (reported missing in action, July 2, 1863; recorded at War Dept., as died July 3, 1863).

Company E:

Privates David Daley (reported missing in action, July 3, 1863; supposed dead), Jacob Miller (reported missing in action, July 3, 1863; supposed dead).

Company H:

Private William Halsey (reported missing in action, July 2, 1863; supposed dead).

Company I:

Private John Disborough (reported missing in action, July 2, 1863; supposed dead).

Mortally Wounded in Action:

Field and Staff:

Major Philip J. Kearny (died August 9, 1863, New York City).

Company A:
Corporal Tyler L. Haring (died July 4, 1863, in field hospital).

Company B:
Privates John H. Rue (died July 19, 1863, in field hospital); Benjamin F. Jackson (died July 7, 1863); Jacob Van Pelt (died at Baltimore, July 9, 1863).

Company E:
Sergeant Eliphalet Sturdevant (died July 13, 1863 in field hospital from complications of amputation of left leg and right arm).

Company G:
Corporal Israel Nixon (died August 2, 1863; U. S. Army General Hospital, Baltimore, Md.).

Company I:
Corporals James P. Stryker (died July 2, 1863; U. S. Army General Hospital, Gettysburg, Pa., of wounds), John W. Joline (died August 17, 1863; Jarvis U. S. Army General Hospital, Baltimore, Md.); Private Silas D. Clark (died July 2, 1863; Gettysburg, Pa.).

Severely Wounded in Action:

Field and Staff:
Colonel Robert McAllister.

Company A:
First Sergeant Joseph Burns; Privates Henry McMahon, Robert E. Mayo (arm amputated), William H. Weaver, Archibald Patton, Daniel Snyder, and Hiram Martin.

Company B:

First Lieutenant William S. Provost.

Company C:

Second Lieutenant John B. Faussett; Privates John Linsey, Franklin Armstrong, James K. Webb, John Crane, Charles Stevenson, and Peter Cougle.

Company E:

Corporals Benjamin Joiner, Absalom Talmadge; Privates Charles Bowman, Samuel Morse.

Company F:

First Lieutenant Edward R. Good; Corporals John F. Bartine, Edward White, Charles Dilks, and George Morton; Privates Edward Powers, William H. Calhoun, and Ephraim Robbing.

Company G:

Sergeant F. W. King; Corporals George Halloway; Privates Charles Koenig, Smith H. Eldridge, Thomas Lowry, George A. McGuire, George F. Seaver, William Emmons, Abijah Thomson, and John W Lloyd.

Company H:

Second Lieutenant William E. Axtell; Sergeant John V. Lanterman; Privates Patrick King, John J. Sites, John C. Nutt, Bartley Owen, and Joseph L. Decker.

Company I:

Corporal Richard J. Merrill; Privates George Chamberlain, Jacob L. Chevalier, James Finnons, Francis Wassimer, William H. Luce, John M. Errickson, Alfred Barcalow, Henry L. Mollison, and Daniel J. Buckley.

Company K:

Corporal Edward Appleton; Privates Amnon J. Foote, John Ardner, Gershom J. Forate, Frederick Soldner, and William Carson (leg amputated).

Slightly Wounded in Action:

Field and Staff:

Adjutant John Schoonover.

Company A:

Corporal Emilie Wappenstein; Privates Emmet Burk, Christopher Snyder, George H. Johnson, and Isaac Harlow.

Company B:

First Sergeant William Hand; Privates John Voorhees, Andrew Webster.

Company C:

Sergeant David Schaffer; Corporal Amos Rockhill; Private Richard V. Howell.

Company D:

Corporal Emanuel Runyon; Privates Richard Burtrone, Edward Spellman, and Theodore Beatty.

Company E:

Sergeant William Egan; Corporal Elise F. Rose; Privates James F. Gibson, Edward J. Kinney, James King, Thomas Scattergood, John Wilson, and Joseph Walton.

Company F:

Captain William H. Lloyd; First Sergeant Benjamin F. Moorehouse; Sergeants Thomas S. White and James C. White; Privates James Thomson, William Collins, and Miller H. Lewis.

Company G:

Sergeant O. F. Holloway; Privates Chapman Marcellus, Thomas Foutch, Thomas Kelly, and Joseph Fowler.

Company H:

Privates Joshua Barber, Timothy K. Pruden.

Company I:

Sergeant Thomas J. Thompson; Corporals E. W. Robinson, Michael Coony; Private Stacy Babcock.

Company K:

First Sergeant Charles C. Reilly; Private John Labort.

Desertions

Company D:

Private George Burnell, July 3, 1863; transferred from Co. B.

Company E:

Private Augustus Francisco, July 14, 1863, at U. S. Army General Hospital, Gettysburg, Pa.

NEW JERSEY UNITS ACTIVELY ENGAGED AT GETTYSBURG[8]

	Engaged Strength	Killed	Wounded	Missing/ Captured	Regimental Total	Percentage	Ranking
Infantry							
5th	206	13	65	16	94	46%	2
6th	207	1	32	8	13	20%	6
7th	275	15	86	13	114	41%	3
8th	170	7	38	2	47	28%	4
11th*	275	21	124	6	153	56%	1
12th	444	23	83	9	115	26%	5
13th	347	1	20	0	21	6%	9
Totals	1,924	80	448	57	585	30%	
Artillery							
Battery A	98	2	7	0	9	9%	8
Battery B	131	1	16	3	20	15%	7
Totals	229	3	23	3	29		
Cavalry							
1st NJ Cavalry	199	0	9	0	9	5%	10
Totals	2,352					26%	

Figures for the 11th NJ in Busey and Martin do not totally agree with those given by Marbaker in his regimental history.

Percentage of Casualties for Infantry Alone Actively Engaged: 30%

Totals of NJ Units Actively Engaged: 2,352

Total Percentage of Casualties for NJ Units Actively Engaged: 26%

[8] From *Regimental Strength and Losses at Gettysburg,* Busey and Martin, 2006.

James H. Lamason with Gerard E. Mayers

The Vortex of Fire Twins

(The 5th NJ and the 11th NJ Together)

Killed	Wounded	Missing/Captured	Total	Percentage
33	189	24	246	51%

Maps of Positions Held at Gettysburg
BY THE ELEVENTH NEW JERSEY

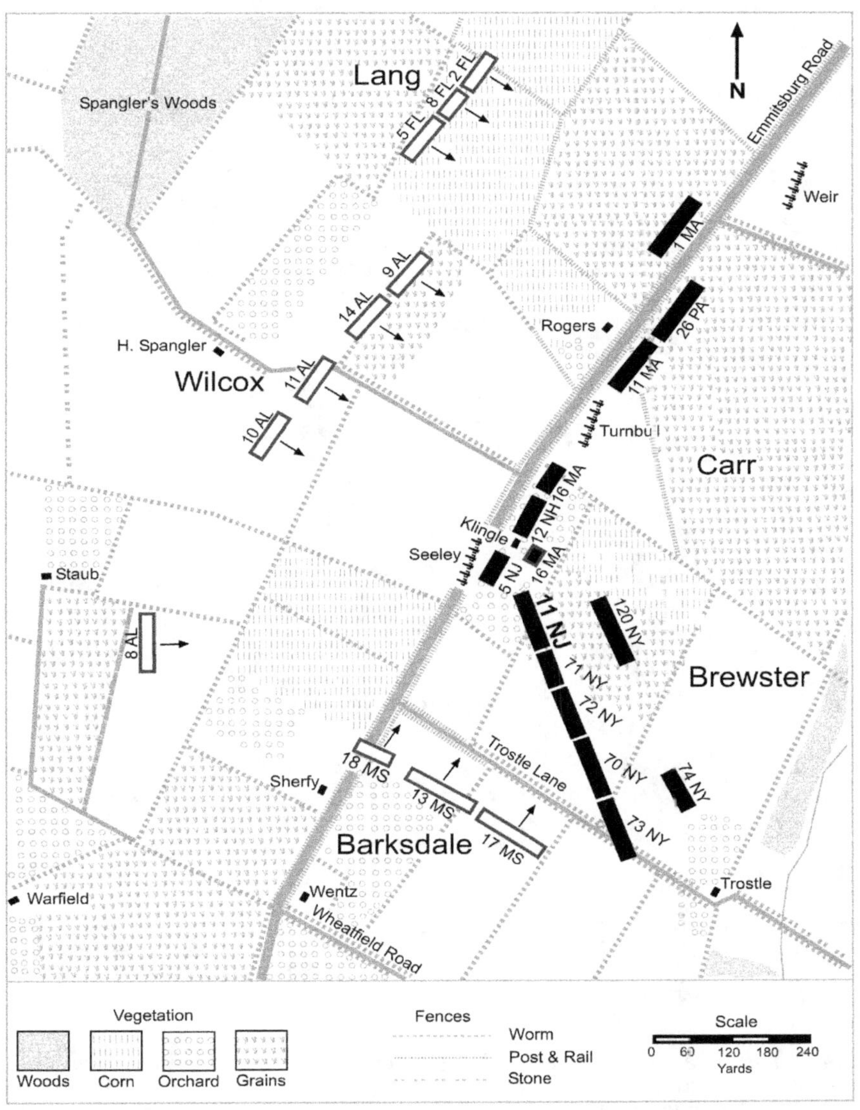

The "salient" formed by Carr's and Brewster's brigades of Humphrey's division of the Third Corps begins to come under attack from Wilcox's Alabama brigade (across the Emmitsburg Road from the Klingel farm) and three regiments of Barksdale's Mississippi brigade, July 2, 1863. Note the positions of Seeley's battery as well as the 5th NJ, the 12th NH, the 120th NY, and the 11th NJ. (Note: While map above spells "Klingle" for the farm, we have used "Klingel" as that is how the iron identification plaque at the Gettysburg National Military Park spells the name.)

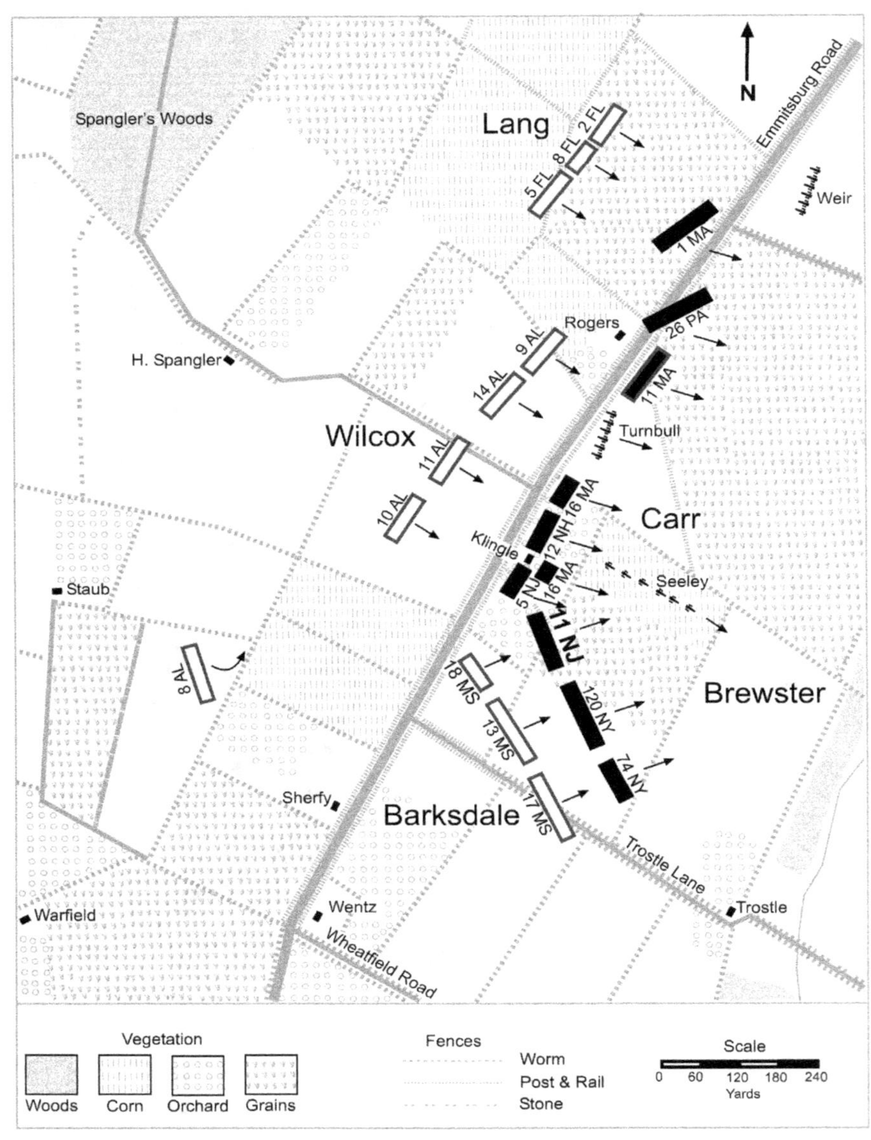

Carr's and Brewster's brigades of Humphrey's division of the Third Corps begin to collapse under attack from Wilcox's Alabama brigade (across the Emmitsburg Road from the Klingel farm) and three regiments of Barksdale's Mississippi brigade, July 2, 1863. Seeley's battery has already pulled out and is retreating back towards the main line of the Army of the Potomac on Cemetery Ridge. From the map, it appears the main antagonist against the Eleventh NJ is Barksdale's Eighteenth Mississippi. Survivors of both brigades retreat back to the safety of the main Union line along Cemetery Ridge. (Note: While map above spells "Klingle" for the farm, we have used "Klingel" as that is how the iron identification plaque at the Gettysburg National Military Park spells the name.)

Photograph of Brevet Major General Robert McAllister, with signature, as found in the front piece of Thomas D. Marbaker's history of the Eleventh Regiment, New Jersey Volunteer Infantry. The photo was used to help sculpt McAllister's face for the burial monument at his grave in Belvidere, New Jersey. (See photo on next page.)

The memorial to Bvt. Major General Robert McAllister at the front of his grave, located in the cemetery in Belvidere, New Jersey. The monument bears testimony to McAllister's courage as well as his strong and profound Christian faith. The sculpture of McAllister is the same as the photo on the previous page. (Photo by James H. Lamason)

The monument to the Eleventh Regiment, New Jersey Volunteers, situated just off Steinwher Avenue (Emmitsburg Road) near the Klingel farmstead. Sculpted by the Smith Granite Company in the shape of a regimental ledger, the monument was commissioned by the state of New Jersey. It was dedicated on June 20, 1888, by John Schoonover, late Lieutenant Colonel of the Eleventh. (Photo by James H. Lamason)

Thoughts and Acknowledgments

T H E G E N E S I S O F this book spans a lifetime. It began when one of my siblings pulled me into helping her with her junior high history project. The project consisted of the opening act of the Civil War, the shelling of Fort Sumter in the harbor of Charleston, South Carolina. The project required the building of a model of the event, creating a report, and then as a family visiting the historical site. So here I was at age nine helping to make the model of the Charleston, S.C. harbor with a miniature Fort Sumter, the surrounding forts, and then the city itself. I then walked onto the parade ground at Fort Sumter. I still remember doing that like it was yesterday!

The other item that spurred my interest in the Civil War was receiving my first book, the *American Heritage Young Readers' Book of the Civil War*. The narration was written by Bruce Catton. Also, between the ages of nine through twelve, I read the Civil War centennial trilogy authored by Mr. Catton. Those three books, plus *This Hallowed Ground* (also by Mr. Catton), pulled me in further.

Time marched on, and so did life. But the events surrounding this time in our nation's history never left the depths of my being. There was something to those eventful four years that continued to intrigue me.

Much like any young person of the day, this obsession ebbed and flowed. High school, college, career, loves, then marriage and children—all became a part of what is me today. However, the desire to learn more about those pivotal four years of our history never left me. As I got older, it dawned on me *why*. In typical American fashion, this nation, this society, this people had to work out its societal differences in its own way.

Who we are as a people, I believe, is why it happened. The result was the most vicious, horrible, passionate way we could settle a major societal difference. That's why we fought the Civil War. Though nothing about it was ever civil, there were times during the beginning of the conflict, when there was still a bit of chivalry.

Then, in the span of a decade, it all was fanned into a passion. A roaring fire where I had to know more. I mean, I *had* to know more!!!

First was the discovery of my wife's relationship to a forgotten major player in the war. G. K. Warren. (That has turned into another work altogether.)

Then two more events. First was a chance meeting with someone (I have an idea of who it was). The conversation went something along these lines: Where are you from? "New Jersey," was my reply. In response, I heard: "Oh, they didn't do anything here (at Gettysburg); they had only 15% casualties!" This set alarm bells off in my brain! I knew my home state had done more than just rest on their weapons and drink coffee—as this woman put it. I had to know more.…And that's where the discovery of the Eleventh New Jersey comes from.

Second, I went through a horrible time of working through a major bout of depression. A life of working, living, marriage, relationships had all taken a toll. And I needed to refocus. I needed to re-center myself. Since I am a man of faith in God and his son Jesus Christ, I leaned on the Bible, prayer, counseling, and yes—even my research and learning. This led me to the discovery of the colonel of the Eleventh New Jersey: Robert McAllister.

Though Colonel McAllister and I differ theologically on some viewpoints of faith, I feel we are kindred spirits. Mc, as I have come to call him and as you will discover, was a man "on in years for his day." One historian of the late 19th and early 20th centuries put it best: "When men of his age should be home with their families enjoying grandchildren and the later duties of life, he forsook it all, and answered the call of duty, honor, and country." McAllister answered that call.

Over the next four years, McAllister served with distinction, with his faith on his sleeve. His ability to survive, and even *thrive,* in this nightmare is such an inspiration.

The other personality and the center piece of this story is John Schoonover. The discovery of him, and his connection to McAllister, looms large in this story.

Others are Andrew Ackerman, Philip Kearny, Surgeon Edward Welling, Captain Samuel Sleeper, and the Irish commissary sergeant who seems to be in every Civil War unit. While documentation on them all is limited to the biographical sketches in Thomas Marbaker's regimental history on the Eleventh, and also as found in John Y. Foster's *New Jersey's Men in the War of Rebellion*, I (and my co-author Gerry Mayers) have tried to be as close to their personalities as the records now available have shown them to be. Time will surely reveal even more on them, as more of recorded history comes to life.

There are two more personalities the reader will meet in this story. In one way, one of them never lived; in another way, he did. I speak of Jacob Mount. He represents all the other men of the regiment of whom we know so little. Yes, it's my attempt to convey to the reader how close I have grown to this band of brothers — and how much I have become a part of them.

Finally, there is a person in this work who *did* live. You have met him previously in the pages of this book. I speak of Lieutenant William J. Mount. Originally from New Shrewsbury, New Jersey, he moves to Freehold, New Jersey, shortly before the war. He musters in as a sergeant in the Third New Jersey Militia (three months) at the beginning of the war. When the Eleventh is mustered in on August 18, 1862, he is listed as a private in Co. A. He then is promoted to sergeant major on September 1, 1862. This rank is the senior-most of all the non-commissioned officers of any regiment of the Civil War. The non-commissioned officers, especially the sergeant majors, are the backbone of every army. Informed speculation exists between the authors that he may have been an acting sergeant major during the Camp Perrine period. Genealogical research has shown that I am related to him. The "how" I cannot pin down exactly. I call it a soft connection, as the research is not definitive as we go to press with this.

When it comes to the actual historical events, my co-author and I have made every attempt to be as close to what is documented as happening. When the record of events is vague, we have tried to use the personalities of the people who experienced it to fill out the story. As a result, this book is as accurate as we could possibly make it. As with any worthy work of historical fiction, we have taken historically based literary license. The conversations set down in this book may or may not have actually taken place. Therefore, any errors are ours and ours alone.

And so, what you hold in your hands is the final product after many reviews and copy edits by several excellent folks. Throughout the entire editing process, my co-author and I read the manuscript many times. To this day, the story still continues to grab at *us*, the authors. As we read each successive draft, we found ourselves asking *Why?* How can a fictional account of actual historical events reach down into the depths of our souls and make us weep? We think it's for two main reasons.

This book originally began as a tactical study of the events surrounding the desperate fight of Carr's Brigade of A. A. Humphrey's division (Second Division, First Brigade) of the Third Corps of the Army of the Potomac. With the Eleventh New Jersey as its core, the study was going to use the Klingel farm as well as detailing each of the units involved.

Then, within the space of about an eighteen-month period, several professionally written books on the actions on July 2, 1863 from the Peach Orchard north through the Klingel farm and the surrounding areas were published. That made us change our focus. Realizing this would be my first published work, I talked to several friends whom I respect highly. All—including my co-author—recommended my crafting a quality work of historical fiction. I gave their suggestions much thought. I realized I'd grown so close to this particular unit during my research and countless battlefield visits. It dawned on me I *could* tell their story; I *had* to tell their story…this way.

One of the other reasons for my telling their story this way is the monument itself to the Eleventh New Jersey. Once you look at it in person, you realize it's in a shape of a book or a ledger. Civil War units used an exceptionally large ledger to record all the information on the unit. Who had mustered in with it? Who was killed or wounded? Who died from disease or even deserted? The other interesting aspect about the monument is that it records who was promoted to what position. Schoonover's incredible rise from a mere private in the First New Jersey, to Commissary Sergeant with that unit, and then his becoming a First Lieutenant and Adjutant of the Eleventh with a subsequent promotion to Lieutenant Colonel following Gettysburg, is chronicled. The monument is that ledger etched in stone, recording for all time the lives of the men who served in it. That stone monument, paid for by the state of New Jersey, tells us — even *shouts* to us — that these ordinary men did extraordinary things.

As with any literary work, a lot of thank you's are necessary. We owe so much to so many for this project. We have always found it interesting that when folks thank their loved ones — they save it for last.

Jim wishes to extend his thanks to:

First, kudos to my wife Beverly. Thank you for your encouragement, for managing the house as I tried to get this done. Your proofreading skills have been beyond compare. To you, a special thank you.

To our son Steven, a history major in his own right, his keen eye for graphics design, his encouragement, and ability to let his father run things by him. Thank you!

To Heather, our daughter. Your love and support, but also your sound counsel and sense of business has helped me to stay the course.

To my dear friend Ed Myskosky, thank you for your input and feedback on the combat scenes, giving me an understanding of how chaotic combat actually was. Your ability to bring your twentieth century experience to the nineteenth century has been a great help. Thank you, my friend!

To my extended family, especially the late Aunt Helen Tyson, whose willingness to share the story of Gouverneur Kemble Warren fanned a glowing ember to know more about one of the more forgotten generals of this period of our history.

To Sherry Warren Reed, Beverly's cousin who continued to prod me to get this done. Her thirst to know more also served as a driving force to finish this.

I owe a debt to so many others. Dear friends Duane and Lori Ann Siskey, Gerry and Bette Mayers, and Todd Heller—all were so encouraging and helpful along the way. I owe an especial debt to my collaborator and co-author, Gerry Mayers. His detailed knowledge of how a Civil War regiment reacted to commands was essential to understanding how they lived, worked, and fought.

To my dear friends, Pastor Steve Nash and Dr. Jeffrey Danco—especially to Dr. Danco, one of my dearest friends and mentor. Thank you both!

To all the gang of the old Civil War Discussion Group—Rick Allen, Mark Wade, Gary McGinnis, Mindy Eckler, Allan Shikvarg, Linda Sanson, the late Dick "Shotgun" Weeks, and so many others. To those whom I have forgotten, my apologies. You know who you are and how you helped.

I also owe a huge debt to two professional historians whom I'm humbled to know. I speak of J. David Petruzzi and of Eric J. Wittenberg. Eric gave me my first chance to share what I had learned about the Eleventh New Jersey at Gettysburg during a battlefield walk. Both gentlemen helped me to focus on how this project would be done.

I would be remiss if I didn't thank the late Teresa Mulchay Letter and Linda Guy. Both had family in this regiment. They shared willingly what they knew of them, and also photos of reunions of the regiment.

To Scott Mingus Sr., whose counsel and insight into writing this, and using the reference material correctly was of great assistance. I too wish to thank him for contributing the profoundly moving Foreword to this work.

To Lonnie Cryan, who lit the fire to know more about Schoonover, and then McAllister. Lonnie also pointed out to me where both McAllister and Schoonover lived. Thank you, Lonnie!

To Scott Hartwig, and John Heiser, who helped me to get going with this project. To Gettysburg Licensed Battlefield Guides Ralph Siegel, Bill Trelease, Chris Army, Michael Waricher and his beloved wife Jenn, Jonathan Krepps, John Hinckleman, Gary Kross, Jim Hessler, and Christina "Tina" Moon, the late Stan McDonell (who once told me he wanted to see me in the Guide room one day), and as well the late Wayne Wachsmuth: you all have been so helpful along the way.

I owe an extremely huge debt to Mr. John Schoonover of Wilmington, Delaware. He is the great-grandson of Colonel John (as the family knows him). His sharing of the personal records of the Colonel and also family stories passed down through time were essential to understanding the life and personality of Colonel John.

To all the staff of the New Jersey State Archives. Their patience was, I am sure, tried to depths of their beings as they tolerated every whoop of discovery as I poured over the papers of the Eleventh New Jersey. Their collective encouragement to press on inspired me enormously when I got overwhelmed.

I also owe a huge debt to the helpful staff of the Archibald S. Alexander Library at Rutgers University in New Brunswick, N.J. That is where the McAllister papers are located, as well as the actual projectiles that wounded him during the Battle of Gettysburg.

To the staff of the Warren County library who graciously helped me. To Joseph Bilby and the staff of the New Jersey National Guard Museum at Sea Girt, New Jersey, who helped me and guided me.

To my friends and comrades in service; my own special band of brothers. I refer to the men of the New Jersey Civil War Heritage Association. Among them are: Tom Burke, Bruce Sirak, Norm Dykstra, Jim Madden, Bob Costello, John Kuhl, John St. Peters, Joe Bilby, Jonathan Kinney, and all the rest of the trustees. Thanks, guys! This is in addition to an excellent past president of the organization and whom I regard as New Jersey's Civil War historian, Dr. David Martin. A successful author in his own right. Thank you, Doc, for your encouragement and friendship as well.

I also owe a thanks to Hugh Brennan, Bruce Crelin, Jeffery Rodriquez, Joel Baker and his son Harry, George Cavalonne and all the others in the Civil War living history community. They, too, shared their collective knowledge of weapons, tactics, order of drill, and the Manual of Arms.

In closing, to the men of the Eleventh Regiment, New Jersey Volunteers: My prayer is that I have done you justice. That this book will spur a new generation of Civil War historians to want to know more about you, your service, and your sacrifices. To you—a tip of the hat and a heartfelt salute, a thank you! And if it is God's will, someday I can sit around a camp-fire in Heaven, drink coffee, and we can share stories. I know, I know; I can hear my evangelical friends cringe. The Bible is clear in that we will recognize those we know here on earth. Just maybe, *maybe,* that will be our lot. One never knows the mind of God...

My prayer and my hope is that I've made these incredibly brave men come alive. That's so you, the reader, will understand the *what* and the *why* of what they did at Gettysburg on July 2, 1863. And yes, like me (and my co-author), it will become a part of you (I hope) as well.

Jim Lamason
September, 2021

SIMILAR TO MY esteemed co-author James Lamason, I have had an almost lifelong fascination with this pivotal period of our national story. My late parents took me to the Gettysburg battlefield for the first time in the summer between my fifth and sixth grade years in elementary school. That was during the Civil War Centennial. When my late father asked me afterwards what I thought of the battlefield, I shocked him by telling him: "I hated it." I do not now recall what my young brain expected to see. I surmise all the towering monuments then placed on the field, especially the Pennsylvania memorial, may have had something to do with that reaction.

In more recent years, however, I've come to deeply appreciate the courage and sacrifices of the men who crossed in mortal combat those three days of early July, 1863. That is partly due to my becoming both a re-enactor and a living historian of that five-year period of history. My being a re-enactor and a living historian gave me profound insights into how the men of both sides lived, moved, operated, and fought. Another reason would be the many visits I've made over the years, some of them with Jim Lamason, to that field. If you've never been to the Gettysburg National Military Park, you need to go…to understand why men who wore Blue and men who wore Gray gave that "last full measure of devotion." And why the monuments to *both* sides matter!

Like Jim, I also have some thanks to extend.

First, I want to thank two fellow Civil War historians and spiritual brothers for their previous and unforgettable help to my becoming an author. I speak of Jim Lamason and Scott Mingus, Sr. Thank you, guys, for affording me the incredible privileges of working on book projects with you both!

Second, I want to thank my wife Bette. Thank you for putting up with my many talks and phone conversations with my fellow author of this work, as well as making it possible for me to make runs to Gettysburg. Jim and I have often referred to that locale as "our other home."

Third, I want to extend my profound thanks to all the people whom I've met over the years who have either been re-enactors or living historians (or both) of the Civil War. You know who you are; your passion and love for this period of our history remains an inspiration.

It has been a humbling privilege to be asked by my fellow Civil War historian and spiritual brother, Jim Lamason, to be part of this fictional story about the Eleventh Regiment of New Jersey Volunteers and their experiences at Gettysburg on July 2, 1863. His passion and love for this regiment is evident in these pages. And, in some small measure, it has rubbed off on me as well. Jim and I have spent many hours discussing and talking about the actions of the Eleventh New Jersey before and during their participation in the battle of Gettysburg. Like him, my hope (and prayer) is that you will understand the *what* and the *why* of what they did there. These brave sons of New Jersey stood shoulder-to-shoulder with their comrades from Pennsylvania, New York, and other states on that blood-soaked field. May they never, *ever*, be forgotten!

Three cheers, and a Tiger!

Gerry Mayers
September, 2021

References

Primary Sources

Books

Bachelder, John B. *The Bachelder Papers: Gettysburg in Their Own Words.* 3 Volumes. Transcribed, edited and annotated by David and Audrey Ladd; Introduction by Richard A. Sauers. Dayton: Morningside House, 1994-1995.

Bartlett, Asa. *The History of the Twelfth New Hampshire Regiment of Volunteers in the War of Rebellion.* Concord: Ira C. Evans Printer, 1897.

Billings, John D. *Hardtack and Coffee or The Unwritten Story of Army Life.* Boston: George M. Smith & Co., 1887. (Republished 2001; Scituate: Digital Scanning Inc.)

Casey, Silas, Brigadier General, U.S. Army. *Infantry Tactics, for the Instruction, Exercise, and Manoœuvres of the Soldier, a Company, Line of Skirmishers, Battalion, Brigade, or Corps d'Armée. Volume I. Schools of the Soldier and Company. Instructions for Skirmishers and Music.* New York: D. Van Nostrand, 1862. (Accessed online August 29, 2020; https://firstnebraskain-fantry.files.wordpress.com/2019/02/caseys-drill-manual.pdf.)

Craighill, William P. *The Army Officer's Pocket Companion; Principally Designed for Staff Officers in the Field.* New York: D. Van Nostrand, 1862. (Republished 2002; Mechanicsburg: Stackpole Books.)

Depuyster, William. *Biographical Sketch of General Robert McAllister.* Archibald S. Alexander Special Collection. New Brunswick: Rutgers Library, Rutgers University.

Duffy, James N., Gottfried Krueger, William H. Corbin, commissioners. *Final Report of the Gettysburg Battle-Field Commission of New Jersey.* Trenton: John L. Murphy Publishing Company, 1891.

Foster, John Y. *New Jersey and the Rebellion: A History of the services of the troops and people of New Jersey in aid of the Union cause.* Published by Authority of the State. Newark: Martin R. Dennis & Co., 1868.

Hardee, W. J., Brevet Lt. Col. *Hardee's Rifle and Light Infantry Tactics, for the Instruction, Exercises and Manœuvers of Riflemen and Light Infantry.* New York: J. O. Kane, 1862. (Republished 1997; Decatur: Invictus, division of Johnson Graphics.)

Marbaker, Thomas E. *History of the Eleventh New Jersey Volunteers: from its organization to Appomattox: to which is added experiences of prison life and sketches of individual members.* Trenton: MacCrellish & Quigley, book and job printers, 1898. (Republished 1991; Hightstown: Longstreet House.)

McAllister, Robert. *The Civil War Letters of General Robert McAllister,* edited by James I. Robertson, New Brunswick: Rutgers University Press, 1965.

O'Shaughnessy, Alonzo. *Alonzo's War, Letters from a Young Civil War Soldier.* Edited by Mary Searing O'Shaughnessy. Rutherford: Fairleigh Dickinson University Press (co-published with The Rowman & Littlefield Publishing Group Inc.), 2012.

Scott, Robert N., *et al. The War of the Rebellion: A Compilation of the Official Records of the Union and Confederate Armies.* Washington, D.C.: Government Printing Office, 1880-1901.

Stryker, William S. *Record of Officers and Men from New Jersey in the Civil War, 1861-1865.* 2 volumes. Adjutant-General's Office. Trenton: John L. Murphy, Steam Book and Job Printer, 1876. "Published by authority of the Legislature." (Accessed online August 29, 2020; https://wwwnet-dos.state.nj.us/DOS_ArchivesDBPortal/StrykerCivilWar.aspx)

Newspapers

The Belvidere Apollo. Belvidere, N.J.: March 6,1891
The Daily News of Stroudsburg, Pennsylvania. Stroudsburg, Pa.: April 13, 1930

Diaries and Letters

The McAllister Collection – Archibald S. Alexander Special Collection. New Brunswick, N.J.: Rutgers Library, Rutgers University.
Schoonover, John. *The Private Diaries.* Unpublished. Courtesy of Mr. John Schoonover, the great-grandson of "Colonel John"; Wilmington, Delaware.

Archives

The New Jersey State Archives, Department of State; Trenton, New Jersey:
The Regimental records of the First New Jersey Regiment of Volunteers.
The Regimental records of the Fifth New Jersey Regiment of Volunteers.
The Regimental records of the Eleventh New Jersey Regiment of Volunteers.
Microfilm records of newspapers and Civil War Pension records of the men from New Jersey in the War of the Rebellion.

Secondary Sources

Bilby, Joseph G., *Small Arms at Gettysburg*. Chicago: Westholme, 2007.

Catton, Bruce, *Terrible Swift Sword (Centennial History of the Civil War)*, 2 vols. Garden City: Doubleday, 1963.

Ferguson, Ernest B., *Chancellorsville 1863: The Souls of the Brave*. New York: Alfred A. Knopf, 1992.

Gindlesperger, James and Suzanne. *So You Think You Know Gettysburg? (Volume 2)*, Winston-Salem: John F. Blair, Publisher, 2014.

Gottfried, Bradley. *The Maps of Gettysburg: Atlas of the Gettysburg Campaign, June 3–July 13, 1863*. El Dorado Hills: Savas Beatie, 2007.

Hessler, James, *Sickles at Gettysburg: The Controversial Civil War General Who Committed Murder, Abandoned Little Round Top, and Declared Himself the Hero of Gettysburg*. El Dorado Hills: Savas Beatie, 2009.

Laino, Philip, *Gettysburg Campaign Atlas*. 3rd edition. Gettysburg: Gettysburg Publishing LLC, 2015.

Martin, David. G., *New Jersey at Gettysburg Guidebook*. Hightstown: Longstreet House, 2012.

Pfanz, Harry, *Gettysburg: The Second Day*. Chapel Hill: University of North Carolina Press, 1987.

Schulz, David L. and Scott L. Mingus, Sr., *The Second Day at Gettysburg: The Attack and Defense of Cemetery Ridge, July 2, 1862*. El Dorado Hills: Savas Beatie, 2015.

Other Sources

Battlefield walks with Gettysburg Licensed Battlefield Guides Bill Trelease, Gary Kross, Jonathan Krepps, John Archer, and the late Wayne Wachsmuth; Gettysburg, Pennsylvania.

Emails and conversations with Dr. David G. Martin.

Emails and conversations with John Schoonover, the great-grandson of "Colonel John;" Wilmington, Delaware.

Emails and conversations with John Heiser, retired Chief Librarian of Gettysburg National Military Park; Gettysburg, Pennsylvania.

Conversations with Scott Hartwig, retired Chief Historian of Gettysburg National Military Park; Gettysburg, Pennsylvania.

Personal messages and emails with Scott Mingus Sr., Author and historian; York, Pennsylvania.

Personal messages, emails, and conversations with co-author Gerard Mayers; co-author (with Scott L. Mingus, Sr.), *Erin Go Bragh: Human Interest Stories of the Irish in the American Civil War, 1861-1865.* Gettysburg Publishing, LLC.; 2018) and Civil War re-enactor/living historian; Milford, New Jersey.

Private messages, conversations, and emails with Ralph Siegel, Licensed Battlefield Guide; Gettysburg, Pennsylvania.

About the Authors

James "Jim" Lamason had his first experience with the American Civil War at age nine, when a sister "recruited" him to help with her junior high history project. He cites the *American Heritage Young Readers' Book of the Civil War*, with narrative written by Mr. Bruce Catton, as spurring on his youthful interest. Catton's Civil War centennial trilogy, plus a companion book *This Hallowed Ground*, pulled him in further. Similar to his co-author/collaborator Gerard "Gerry" Mayers, the Ken Burns mini-series *The Civil War* and the Ted Turner Pictures *Gettysburg* movie rekindled his interest. A discovery of his wife being a relation to Civil War general G. K. Warren during a family get-together contributed to his interest and in becoming a true passion to learn more of this period.

He has researched, studied, and read about the Eleventh Regiment of New Jersey Volunteers for over fifteen years. During that time, he has also been involved with the New Jersey Civil War Heritage Association. In that organization, he served a three-year term as president; he has also been (and continues as) a trustee.

As with his wife, Lamason has ancestors who served in the Civil War. In addition to Lt. William J. Mount mentioned in this book, he is related to Pvt. John Dougherty, Thirtieth New Jersey Volunteers; to Pvt. Samuel Gillespie, Thirty-third New Jersey Volunteers; to Cpl. Ezekiel Pope, Second Pennsylvania Heavy Artillery; to Pvt. Jacob

Lamason, First Pennsylvania Reserves/Twentieth Pennsylvania Cavalry (step-two times great-grandfather); and to Jedediah Hotchkiss, mapmaker for Confederate Major General Thomas J. "Stonewall" Jackson (five times great-uncle). Recently retired after a career in IT for financial institutions and then in retail with Home Depot, he lives with his wife Beverly and son Steven in Middlesex, New Jersey.

Gerard "Gerry" Mayers has been a life-long Civil War buff but credits both the Ken Burns mini-series *The Civil War* and the Ted Turner Pictures *Gettysburg* movie with rekindling his interest. He holds degrees in both English and History (with Honors) from St. John's University, New York. Active with the Bucks County Civil War Roundtable (Doylestown, Pa.), he is the program chairman for that organization as well as an At-Large Member of its Board of Directors. He is also involved with Civil War reenacting and living history. An alumnus member of the Civil War Heritage Foundation (where he portrayed John W. Fairfax of Lt. General James Longstreet's staff), he currently belongs to Company C, 44th Regiment, Georgia Volunteer Infantry as a re-enactor. In that organization, he portrays a member of the original Company C of the regiment.

Mayers has previously published an historical fiction novel about the Confederate side of the September 1862 Maryland Campaign, culminating in the horror that was Antietam/Sharpsburg. Titled *None But Heroes*, the book is presently available on Amazon Kindle. (A companion novel, dealing with the Union side of the same campaign, remains in the works.) This book is his second historical fiction project. In conjunction with Scott Mingus, Sr., he co-authored *Erin Go Bragh: Human Interest Stories of the Irish in the American Civil War, 1861-1865*.

Mayers's maternal two times great-grandfather, Patrick Bracken, was a veteran of the Mexican-American War; his maternal great-grandfather James T. Bracken served with Battery E, First N.J. Light Artillery; and his maternal great-granduncle John G. Bracken served with the Twenty-first Regiment, N.J. Volunteer Infantry, Co. A. (Both James and John were proud first generation Irish-Americans.)

He is married to his wife Bette. They reside in the charming upper Hunterdon County/Delaware River town of Milford, New Jersey.